SUSAN HILL

Susan Hill has been a professional writer for over fifty years. Her books have won awards and prizes including the Whitbread, the John Llewellyn Rhys and the Somerset Maugham; and have been shortlisted for the Booker. She was awarded a CBE in the Queen's Diamond Jubilee Honours. Her novels include *Strange Meeting, I'm the King of the Castle, In the Springtime of the Year* and *A Kind Man.* She has also published autobiographical works and collections of short stories as well as the Simon Serrailler series of crime novels. The play of her ghost story *The Woman in Black* has been running in London's West End since 1988. She has two adult daughters and lives in North Norfolk.

SUSAN HILL

From the Heart

VINTAGE

1 3 5 7 9 10 8 6 4 2

Vintage
20 Vauxhall Bridge Road,
London SW1V 2SA

Vintage is part of the Penguin Random House group of companies
whose addresses can be found at global.penguinrandomhouse.com.

Penguin
Random House
UK

First published in Vintage in 2018
First published in hardback by Chatto & Windus in 2017

penguin.co.uk/vintage

A CIP catalogue record for this book is available from the British
Library

ISBN 9781784706135

Printed and bound by Clays Ltd, St Ives plc

Penguin Random House is committed to a sustainable future
for our business, our readers and our planet. This book is made
from Forest Stewardship Council® certified paper.

MIX
Paper from
responsible sources
FSC® C018179

From the Heart

I

EVELYN PIPER had prayed for a family of three sons, only to be disappointed by giving birth to a single daughter. Olive was a calm and peaceful baby, a contented child and a pleasant, rather self-contained girl, and at every stage had the knack of being liked, but was never able to believe that this was the case.

Her mother had wanted compensation for producing just one child, a girl, by her being, at the very least, a beauty. But Olive had a plain face and by the age of fourteen she was short-sighted and so hid it behind large spectacles, which made her look startled. In fact, when it had settled into its adult form, she was attractive, simply because her natural expression was one of open friendliness. She had a perfect skin, silk-smooth when others suffered from varying degrees of acne, and her brown eyes were both warm and intelligent. But the large glasses did a good job of hiding all that, too.

'Whoever would be drawn to you?'

Olive was not unhappy with the implied answer, and if young men were not drawn to her, friends were. There was everything to like about her. She was a sympathetic listener, she was good-tempered and she had a certain shy wit. She was interested in things. She grasped things. She was tactful and truthful, and she did not tell tales.

And all the time her mother, though always loving her, could find nothing about her daughter in which to take pride.

Evelyn Piper died suddenly when Olive was seventeen and preparing for her A levels.

An unexpectedly large number of people came to the funeral, most of whom Olive did not know, though some she recognised – neighbours, a cousin. But others, all women, came from the Townswomen's Guild, to which Evelyn had belonged. She had led an active social life during lunch hours and in the afternoons, though had said little to her family about it, and in the evenings had rarely ventured out except to the local repertory theatre, two or three times a year, with her husband Ralph – she had despised the cinema – and twice a year to Ladies' Night at the Masonic Lodge.

'I'm glad we decided to do the tea,' Olive said to her father that evening. They were sitting in the small back room overlooking the garden. Her father called it his study, though he only read the paper there, or listened to Light Music programmes, such as the 'Palm Court Orchestra' on the radio. It had been the room his own father had occupied as a study, for this was the house in which he had grown up, and which he had inherited. He had moved back in the year after he had married Evelyn.

The windows were open onto the May garden, and always afterwards the smell of wallflowers brought back that evening of the funeral.

'There was never any question of not giving tea, was there?'

There had been. Twice he had said that he was sure it wouldn't be necessary, that few people would come, so that Olive had almost given up on the idea herself. As it turned out, there had not been enough to eat and too few teacups. She had had to rush about collecting empty ones and washing and replacing them and cutting small cakes up to make smaller ones.

'I'm glad we did it, anyway. People were very appreciative.'

She looked across at her father in profile, sitting in his wing chair, and had not the least idea what he was feeling. She had never known what either of her parents felt, though she had gathered this and that about what they thought.

It was disconcerting. She loved him. He loved her, she knew. Once he had said, with a small smile, that he was very relieved her mother had not got her wish for three sons. But she did not know him.

Of course he had been badly shaken, and deeply upset when it had happened, in such a frighteningly sudden way. Evelyn had been walking in through the garden door, carrying two pots of seedlings, and saying 'I'm still worried about late frosts, you know', and on the 'you know' she had fallen to the ground. Olive had been immediately behind her, Ralph had just come in through the front door, from work, and was hanging his hat on its peg. There had been a soft thud as she had gone down, and then she had simply lain, crumpled and utterly still. Olive had not realised that people could die in that way, walking, talking – dead.

2

I F EVERYONE liked Olive, Margaret Reid liked her in particular, because Olive had defended her against the others after she had been seen in town one Saturday, holding hands with a boy. Word spread, remarks were whispered, glances exchanged.

'She is quite pretty.'

'What has that got to do with it?' Olive had spoken quietly but still silenced the talk.

'Ol, it's got *everything* to do with it!'

'I'm sure it's because he just likes her.'

Sighs. Oh, Olive, honestly. Eye rolls.

'Anyway, more to the point, who saw them? Did you, Olive?'

But she had not.

'So who did? Come on.'

'Loads of people. Sheila. Lois. Penny C.'

'So, where are they?'

But they were all in the Science set and not in the Sixth Form Common Room that morning.

It was still half being talked about when Margaret came in to fetch her music case. The room went quiet. Margaret stood, looking round at them, defiant. But she went red and Olive saw that she was close to tears. She said, 'I think you should leave Margaret alone and probably apologise. She hasn't done anything wrong.'

'How do you –'

'Shut up!' Olive never spoke sharply or raised her voice, but she did so now. And because it was her and everyone liked her, and because her mother had died, they stopped. The afternoon bell rang. People got up. The door swung open and shut, open and shut. After that, the subject was not mentioned again.

'I wouldn't mind,' Margaret said now, across the table with its long white cloth, 'but it's not exactly as if I'm unique. Esther Barrett's been going out with Adrian for three terms.' She had invited Olive to have Saturday-morning coffee and ices with her in the Garden Restaurant at Archer & Saunders, where the smart local women met.

'We should wear hats.'

So Margaret had on a small straw one with an upturned brim and a bunch of mauve artificial flowers. Olive only had a beret. Her mother had worn hats, to the Townswomen's Guild lunches, but she and her father had given them all away, with the rest of her clothes.

'You wouldn't want any of these,' Ralph Piper had said, and it was true. But Olive had felt hurt all the same, wanting to have decided for herself. To her father, she was still seven or eight years old.

She had put the beret on at an angle, and at once heard Evelyn's voice, regretting the large spectacles.

'You would think I could at least have had a daughter with perfect eyesight.'

She and Margaret had a silver pot of coffee, and ices in tall tulip glasses, white pink white pink, in layers, with cochineal syrup running down the sides like blood and wafers set jauntily.

'This is my treat, by the way,' Margaret said. 'My mother gave me extra pocket money for it, when I told her you stood up for me. But anyway, let's not talk about all that.'

Anyone else would have asked about the boy she had been seen out with, but such a question never entered Olive's head.

'I came here with my mother once,' she said, looking round. The restaurant was full. 'I was nine. I knocked my glass of squash all over the tablecloth.'

She could see the vivid orange stain spreading.

Some of it had splashed onto the plate of her mother's friend Irma, soaking the sponge base of her cake. Olive had cried. She had not been brought here again.

'Some Saturdays, there are mannequins. They twirl between the tables with their hands on their hips. They model spring suits and fur stoles.'

Olive was disappointed there were none today.

'We'll come again then.'

Was this the way it came about, the shift from being a girl to being a woman? With coffee and ices in Archer & Saunders which you paid for yourself?

'What are you going to do, Ol? Watch out, you've got red dribbling down your chin. Maybe you should nudge that beret a bit more at an angle . . . do you think? Look in the wall mirrors.'

How did Margaret know all this?

'What do you mean, what am I going to do?'

'A career. Joyce and Sheila are applying to medical school.'

'I know, but both their fathers are doctors.'

'I'm thinking of the WRAF.'

'Whatever for?'

'The men, what else ?'

'Oh.' Olive had never met anyone in the Services.

'Or the Wrens. Only they don't get to go to sea.'

'Do they fly aeroplanes, in the WRAF?'

'Yes. They had to let them, once the war got under way. Too many men had got killed. Like my dad.'

Margaret had only mentioned her father once before. He had been shot down during the Battle of Britain, a month before she was born. When Olive had said that she was sorry, Margaret had shrugged. 'Don't be. I'm not. How can you be sorry for someone you never knew? Tony's the only dad I've ever had.'

Her mother had remarried before the end of the war. How did it feel, Olive thought now, never to have known your real father? To call someone 'Dad' who was not? But it seemed unimportant to Margaret.

Now she stuck her long spoon back in the empty glass.

'Oh, I don't know. I'll probably end up doing shorthand and typing, you know – secretarial college. You can go to London to do that.'

'Do you want to go to London?'

Margaret put her hand on Olive's for a second. 'You are sweet, Oli. I know why I like you.'

'Do you?'

She saw that Margaret had drawn a little tick at the corners of her eyes with black pencil. She had never looked so closely at another girl's face before.

'Sweetie, *everybody* wants to go to London . . . well, of course they do!'

Do I, then? Olive thought.

It was something else that had never occurred to her.

3

'OLIVE – COME in and sit down. Isn't it a beautiful day? Makes me wish we could do all this out in the garden.'

The Careers mistress was the only married teacher in the school which, for some reason they all recognised but could not explain, made her more relaxed with them, and friendlier, less outwardly formal, though she could be as strict as the rest when necessary. She just did not seem to feel it was necessary very often and because she treated the sixth form less like children, more like young women, they behaved well. They liked her. Mrs Pratley – Geography and Careers. But they knew that her name was Alison. They thought of her as Alison. The rest of the staff seemed hardly even to possess Christian names – they were M. L. Philips, E. Pearman, R. J. Black . . .

Why was Mrs Pratley less stiff? Why did she simply seem more human?

They were in the small room off the front hall, sometimes used for waiting visitors. The sun was on the front of the building, making a halo behind Mrs Pratley's fair hair. She leaned back, smiling at Olive. There was even something softer and less formal about the way she dressed – pale blue shirt, navy skirt and a white cardigan slung round her shoulders. Small stud earrings. Lipstick.

'Normal,' someone had once said, when they were discussing her. 'She's just normal and they're not.'

'They are – normal for their type anyway.'

'Exactly.'

What was it? A wedding ring? Was that all the rest of them needed to change them entirely?

'Right, Olive . . . you go first. I'm here to give you any information you may want, or even some ideas. But you probably have plenty of your own.'

'No. No, not really.'

'What, none at all? Don't tell me you're one of those who've "never really thought about it, Mrs Pratley".'

She had thought about it. She had made lists. What she was good at. What she was hopeless at. What she enjoyed. Those were easy enough to compile, but what she could see herself doing for the rest of her life, was not.

'Let's look at some of the more obvious ones then. I doubt if you're nursing material, and in any case, you've only done the basic required sciences. According to Miss Box . . .' She glanced down at a folder open on the desk. Olive saw her own name, upside down, above lists of exam marks, and unreadable teacher comments.

'Miss Box . . . feels you are "sadly lacking in any sense of form or design though your ideas for colour are strong". You don't play an instrument, not in the choir . . . no outstanding sports results. And though I always felt you were politely interested, you did not strike me as any sort of a geographer.' She smiled at Olive, an almost conspiratorial smile. 'Oh dear!'

Olive smiled back. She did not feel challenged in any negative way by Mrs Pratley. She felt that somehow they were on the same side. Otherwise, she realised that she was just happy to be sitting here, as the sun moved round and warmed her arms. She would like to have stayed and talked, not about herself and her future. Just talked.

'It's good to rule things out, Olive . . . what you might call the peripherals.' Mrs Pratley's cardigan was slipping off her shoulder. She hitched it back and the diamond on her engagement ring flashed in the sun.

'So – what is Olive Piper really like? Tell me. What are your strengths, as you see them? What gives you the most pleasure? Does anything interest and inspire you so much that you want to go on with it beyond the point where you need not?'

'Oh yes. Medieval English writers. What they thought, what they wrote. Their language. How their minds worked. And then the Metaphysical poets. We're actually studying the Romantics, Wordsworth and Coleridge and the rest. I hate them – they're . . . they're like pastry.'

Mrs Pratley laughed, showing small, very even teeth. Good teeth. Her lipstick was soft cherry pink, on full lips.

'And then look at poets like John Donne and George Herbert and a poem like "They flee from me that sometime did me seek . . ." and . . . then go back to Chaucer even.'

'I will. You are very well and widely read, Olive . . . you've obviously made the most of the library but even a good grammar school like this hasn't such a range of literature. Do you use the public one?'

'Oh yes. They get me things from the stacks that they don't have on the shelves – and from other libraries. They're so helpful.'

'That's because any librarian loves readers like you. What about Shakespeare? Which plays are your favourites?'

'I don't know them all . . . but *Troilus and Cressida* more than any.'

'*Hamlet*?'

'Yes. We're doing that for A level. I like *Macbeth* better though.'

She became conscious of a difference in the way Mrs Pratley looked at her. Up to this moment she had been interested, but this interview had been like the rest – dig a bit, find out, make some suggestions. Routine. Not Olive.

'And *Cymbeline* . . . and *The Tempest*.'

'You've seen all those?'

'Oh no, only read them. I've only been to the theatre once – *Romeo and Juliet*. We're doing that as well. I hated it.'

Mrs Pratley laughed again. But not at her. Not in that sarcastic way teachers had.

'So. Literature and History. Literature *or* History?'

'Yes. I love them but what could I do with them?'

'Teach them of course! Pass on that love. You have what is worth everything in a teacher – a teacher of any subject – passion. Enthusiasm. Opinions. Knowledge. But enthusiasm most of all. Generations of girls would be so lucky to be inspired by a teacher such as you could become.'

She sat back, still smiling.

'Take my word for it, Olive. It shines out of you. Otherwise, I'll send you off to be a hospital almoner!'

After she had closed the door behind her, Olive found herself for a rare moment completely alone in the long school corridor. It had blue-and-cream tiles set in a line down the middle of terracotta ones, like a carpet runner, and the great brass ship's bell – no longer used and with its rope looped up and tied – gleaming against the polished wood panelling. The smell of polish, and meat and potatoes cooking for dinner. The Honours Boards. The House noticeboards. The Games Teams noticeboards. And in the background, the classroom murmur. The scrape of a chair. Someone coughing.

She stood still and knew that for no particular reason, and for every reason, she would remember this.

Teaching. She supposed it was inevitable. She wondered how she would cope with teaching the things that meant so much to her, that enriched and enlightened and delighted her and made her heart beat faster, to girls who did not want to be taught about them, saw no point. It was the others – however few – those others for whom she would give up everything.

She walked up the stairs to the Common Room, wondering if Mrs Pratley felt any passion for teaching unwilling girls, as Olive herself had been, as they learned to draw maps of the Ruhr coalfield and list the principal industries of North America and construct geological strata from plasticine.

Perhaps, as Mrs Pratley was married, it did not matter so much. Her real life was elsewhere.

4

'I WONDER if you would care to come to Ladies' Night, Olive? Of course, I always took your mother, but where Masons are widowers, you know, daughters or sisters are invited instead. It is quite formal. I don't know how you feel about what you should wear . . . you remember Evelyn's gowns, that sort of thing. She always looked very smart.'

They were sitting over the cheese and biscuits after a supper of kedgeree, which he had cooked. Ralph Piper was a good, plain cook who sometimes liked to experiment. Olive was a poor one, with a limited repertoire, mainly dishes learned in Domestic Science lessons years ago – cauliflower cheese, shepherd's pie. She did not enjoy cooking but she was neat and swift. Her father was a painstaking, fiddly cook and left the kitchen like a bomb site, either for Olive to clear and clean, or for Mrs Bradley the next morning. Mrs Bradley had come once a week in Evelyn's day but now she came three times. Olive knew that it was not only because she was glad of the money. She suspected that it was also because she felt sorry for her, a seventeen-year-old girl living alone with her father.

Olive spread some butter on her cream cracker and topped it in a careful pattern with tiny rectangles of Cheddar, avoiding her father's eye. Masonic Ladies' Night. Something close to panic moved like the sea within her.

'Olive?'

'I'm . . . I'm not sure, honestly. Isn't there someone more suitable you could take?'

'You are very suitable – who better? I understand that it isn't going to be full of lively young people but we do have a very enjoyable evening, the food is quite choice, and there are gifts for the ladies.'

Olive thought of the silver dressing-table set – mirror, brush, clothes brush, comb, tray, backed in petit point. It was still on the chest of drawers in the room where Ralph now slept alone, one of the few things of Evelyn's that he had wanted to keep.

A Ladies' Night gift.

She got up and started to clear away, avoiding the rest of the conversation.

5

THAT YEAR the first weeks of autumn were as
warm as high summer. Schoolchildren started
the new term in cotton frocks and Bedford College
lawns were scattered with people lying spreadeagled,
eyes closed and basking in the sun, or sitting in
groups, talking idly. Or, like Olive, reading in deck-
chairs beneath the great spreading copper beech.
Marlowe was a revelation, so was Webster. Shakespeare
took a back seat for the time being.

Her head teemed with new words and works, so
that not only the lines but the lives, and the truths
told, the golden images and dark metaphors might at
any moment come spilling out and walk about on the
grass. She raised her head, and saw Faustus in black
and the Devil in scarlet.

The Victorian buildings behind her were quiet and

half empty in the afternoon haze. From somewhere behind high hedges, the pock of a tennis ball on racquet and cries of 'Out'. Olive wanted to play. It was the only game she had ever enjoyed and been quite good at, though she over-served and was a clumsy runner. But her hand–eye coordination was excellent. Noticeboards in the hall invited new players, as they invited new actors, singers, folk dancers, bridge players. She had not yet signed up for any of them. There was too much to take on and all at once.

She was glad, now, that she had come to one of the women's colleges of London University – though there were plenty of male tutors. The competition for places at the large, mixed colleges was very strong. Men dominated. There were big faculties of Law and Theology at King's, as well as a Medical School. She would almost certainly waste an application, Mrs Pratley had said.

'Not that I want to put you off if you are really determined, Olive, but honestly, we get very few girls into those. You will get a place at Westfield or Bedford College without any trouble. They'll be lucky to have you.'

All the same, down for the interviews, and with part of a morning free, she had walked through London to look at King's, walked into the court, become caught up in a sudden exodus from lectures, a surge of bodies, men in black gowns, men carrying books, men running. There were women too, but fewer. She had retreated.

Bedford College had been a haven of calm, set in its green gardens, with trees round the lake, courts and playing fields beyond.

She had a room overlooking the park. The sound of traffic was distant, and unheard at night. It might have been in the middle of the country. London was there if she wanted it, but for now she was happy, in a world that seemed to have been made especially for her.

She pieced together the jigsaw, and saw that the picture was in fact quite clear and easy to follow. It was an extension of school, but with fewer rules and people in charge. Young women lived together. Studying, listening, taking notes, meeting and talking, talking, talking. People were no longer so petty. Friendships were formed. People drifted together and apart, but did not seem to fall out explosively, and there was little backbiting. Life was too full, too interesting, for that.

After much thought, Olive joined the Drama Society.

The corners of the garden were thick with leaves. In the early morning, the lake exhaled a fine mist like breath, which dissolved as the sun touched it.

Nights grew colder. Frosts iced the grass. There was the smell of bonfires.

She became embedded in Anglo-Saxon and Middle English and all things Elizabethan. She was required to study the literature of the eighteenth century, tried hard and failed to appreciate it. It seemed to her bland and pompous, against the edginess, spikiness of earlier writers.

Mary Murdoch, with whom she shared her room, had a boyfriend at home in Lincoln. They wrote to one another twice every day. There was always an envelope addressed in his bright blue, looped hand, waiting on the post shelf. She was studying Biological Sciences, he was in Durham doing Theology and preparing for holy orders. They would finish their degrees and marry as soon as she had a teaching post and he a curacy. It was all agreed, sealed and franked. There was a portrait photograph of him on Mary's bedside table – pleasant-looking and somehow already middle-aged, with family and parish responsibilities.

Olive wondered if that would be her before long. Was there some Paul or Roger or Jeremy out there for her, wearing tweed sports jacket and unobtrusive tie? Whenever she tried the idea on for size, as it were, she jumped back, as if she had received a mild electric shock.

Mary's boyfriend, Anthony Whittaker, came down

for the weekend and shook hands with Olive and said that he had heard a lot about her.

'I feel I can trust Mary with you.'

What did he mean? She supposed it meant that she was quiet and wore large glasses and plain skirts and jumpers, and so was safe.

6

THE DEMONS came running out of the bushes and leaped onto the stage that had been erected on the lawns leading down to the lake. They pursued Faustus, dressed in black with a scarlet hood, until, in a much rehearsed and perfectly executed move, he reared up and fell backwards, into the water.

On each of the four nights that the play was performed, warm, beautiful nights, with the floodlights surrounded by deep darkness and the pale moths drawn in to them, on each night, the actor playing Faustus fell in a flawless backwards somersault and there was a gasp, and a thrill rippled through the audience. They sat on tiered platforms high above the stage.

Olive had seen very little real theatre and the performances were a revelation. Forever after, she was

25

to see a lake set in gardens, see Faustus leap, dive, fall, hear the splash. Hear the gasp.

She was the prompt, with the book and a torch, concealed behind laurels, to which at various points various actors crept, to hide and await their cues. She remembered the smell of their excited sweat and the greasepaint, saw wild eyes and crouched bodies, quivering with attention, poised to run out on stage.

No theatre was ever to hold so much for her again.

Waiting to go on for his last scene, and the plunge into the lake, Faustus stood beside Olive, concealed in the laurels. He had not spoken to her, he was too focused and intent, but on the Saturday night, she whispered, 'Last dive,' and he had looked at her as if she were a statue come to life. She had been there every night but somehow invisible. Relaxed now, he adjusted his scarlet hood, and smiled. Conspirators.

It had threatened rain but the clouds had moved off.

She had felt an unreal sense of being next not to a student actor, but to Faustus.

Faustus.

The final somersault. The last cry. The last applause.

Olive closed the book.

His name was Malcolm Crowley and now, in dry clothes, blue shirt and cords, he came over to her at the after-play party. She had been about to leave. The whole *Dr Faustus* time had been the most enjoyable of her life, but she was exhausted, her energy and concentration crashed as he had crashed into the lake.

'Thanks,' he said.

'What for ?'

'Well . . . being there, I suppose.'

'Behind the bush?'

'Yes . . . behind the bush. It was reassuring.'

No one was paying them any attention. Olive drank her wine, which tasted acid-sweet. He was at King's Dental School. His father was a dentist, had been there before him. He was nothing like Faustus. Of course not. It had all been . . . what? What were actors? What were the characters they pretended to be? What happened to them when the lights went down and their costumes were removed? They did not exist. They had never existed. For some reason, she found that disturbing.

Malcolm Crowley.

He smiled at her, raising his glass of beer. And then someone tapped his shoulder.

Speeches. Thanks.

Olive hid her half-full glass behind a lamp and left.

She dreamed about the play. Costumed figures processed across lawns in the fading light. Words floated on the still air. The crackle of applause, losing its impact as it too floated away, without the usual retaining walls of a theatre to bounce it back.

A late blackbird singing. The shout. The backwards fall. The splash.

She held it for days like a box of photographs inside her head.

What next? What next? She was asked for suggestions.

An envelope, by hand, addressed to her, sat on the post shelf.

Hello. Three weeks left. Time flies! I enjoyed our brief encounters. How about another, not so brief? I could meet you in the Goldfish Bowl café – do you know it? Thursday or Friday. We could have a pie and some beer? Or there's Spaghetti House. Whatever you would like.

All best,

Faustus

So this is how it began. She had stepped onto a moving staircase from which she did not know how to alight, though she supposed that the staircase might stop of its own accord at any point. She could not think of any good reason to refuse his invitation.

'You like him, don't you?'

Mary had just washed her hair and was lying on the rug in front of the electric fire to dry it. The room smelled of hot hair.

'Yes. No. I mean, I don't really know him.'

'Of course you don't, but now you will.'

'Will I?'

'Olive, it's what all this is *about.*'

The pub was noisy and full of cigarette smoke. The Spaghetti House was quieter.

'Love this, don't you? Love Italian food. Have you been to Italy?'

'No.'

He had a very fine fair down on his upper cheeks, like the down on a small child's arm. Grey eyes. He was neither tall nor short. Amiable. Trying to please.

She tried back.

She looked at his rather thick fingers, holding knife and fork, and saw them inside a mouth. Felt them inside her own mouth. She had been to the dentist the last time she had been home.

'Will you act in the next play?'

He shook his head. 'Bit close to exams. Maybe the one after that. It takes you out of yourself . . . out of . . . you know.'

'Teeth?'

He laughed loudly, showing his own.

'What is the next play anyway?'

She told him the options she had seen on a list. Not even a longlist, yet.

'Hope it's *The Importance of being Earnest.*'

'You as Ernest?'

'Yes. You'd make a great Miss Prism.'

'Oh no. I wouldn't act. I couldn't. I'd like to direct sometime. Or assistant direct anyway. But anything backstage. Looking on. I love that.'

'Yes. You are a looker-on, aren't you?'

Walking to the Tube station, he put his arm round her. He smelled immensely clean. He bought her ticket. Saw her through the barrier and waited until she was out of sight. Nice manners, her mother would have noted. Her mother had always been impressed by manners. Her mother would have liked him.

It was seven stops, after which she had to catch a bus or walk the last mile. She would walk. She wanted to go over everything. Not what had happened but how she had felt about what had happened, every one of her reactions, for this was as new to her as being born.

The train was quiet. She sat down. An elderly man moved across the carriage to sit opposite her. He wore an old coat and unmatching shoes. She looked at his shoes, still working her way through the evening in her mind, step by step, and as she did so, her eyes travelled up from the old man's unmatching shoes to his sludge-coloured trousers and to his hands, which were on his knees. The knees were splayed apart and tucked in between them, not quite concealed by them, or by the coat, was something she did not recognise or understand, a reddened finger of flesh with its tip flushed purple. She stared and the man moved his hands and then lifted his head and looked her full in the face. In the eyes, before his own eyes somehow directed her to look down again.

She got up and ran, as the train clattered into the next station. It did not matter which station. She left her bag behind her on the seat.

She did not tell anyone what had happened, mainly because she was unsure if anything had. She had been bewildered and frightened. The next day, the College secretary rang the train line.

'It's there,' she said, beaming with pleasure for the anxious-looking girl with large spectacles, in front of her desk. 'It was handed in. You're very lucky.' She gave Olive a slip of paper on which she had written the address and phone number of lost property for their area.

It had been handed in very early that morning, and everything was there, her purse, student card, powder compact and the lipstick she never wore. All there. Handed in by an old man.

J. Smith. They showed her his signature in the book.

She still told no one, not for the rest of her long life, and after a while the whole thing faded and she simply stopped caring about it.

J. Smith.

J. Smith.

J. Smith.

It was a long time before it dawned on her that this was almost certainly not his name.

7

S HE WENT out with Malcolm Crowley four times that term. Mary made sideways remarks. Olive did not say that she went because she was unsure how to refuse. And the evenings were always enjoyable. She liked him. He did not have her interests but they had things in common, small things, and when he held her hand in his own warm one, she felt safe. When he put his arm round her, she smelled his cleanness. It became familiar. When he kissed her, his dry lips pressed together, she – what did she feel? Nothing. Something. She did not want to recoil. She felt – for some reason, the word 'interested' came to her. In the last week of term he asked her to make a visit to his family. The suggestion made her panic but she did not know why. She was safe, wasn't she? This was nice, kind, safe Malcolm Crowley.

She wanted to back away.

On the second weekend of the vacation she took the train to Cheltenham and she might as well have taken it home, for the Crowleys' house was so like her family house, in a similar residential road, detached, with a small front garden and a large back one, with apple trees, overlooking playing fields. Edwardian. Solid. Rooms of the right proportion. A house comfortable in its own bricks and mortar. Fitting. Not imposing, but not reticent either. Olive felt both reassured and strangely disappointed, for she had wanted difference, a challenge even, her horizons expanded. Here they were safely reinforced and bounded, and by the Crowleys, he, larger and heartier than her own father yet still not unlike him. They would have recognised one another.

Malcolm's mother was not like Evelyn Piper. She was shyer, quieter, nicer. She smiled a lot. She merged into the background in a way her mother had never done, and from choice.

It was all very suitable.

Malcolm took her into town in his father's MG sports car, and then on, into the country. Soft low hills. Gentle meadows. Not dramatic country. Nothing to startle.

Olive looked at his face as he drove. How had he come to be chosen as Faustus? Yet he had done it well. Donning the scarlet and black, he had donned the terrible, tragic, doomed figure. Of course, actors were not the characters they played, any more than writers were the characters they invented. And yet . . .

That evening they went, all four of them, to the local theatre to see *The Winslow Boy*.

'Very satisfactory,' Peter Crowley said. 'You see what they mean by "a well-made play".'

'You could have been an actor,' Olive said to Malcolm. But it turned out that acting was not a serious career, acting was a hobby. Hobbies were important though, and he might well join the local amateurs, once he was settled in his work, and life.

'Nice people,' Moira Crowley said. 'You'll meet some really nice people.'

'Isn't that how you two met? Over a prompt book, as it were?'

Peter Crowley took her arm. She did not quite want it, though not because it was in any way unpleasant, but because it seemed somehow too proprietorial. She felt herself being drawn into a place where she was not sure she wanted to be.

They sat drinking a last cup of tea, Malcolm beside her with his arm along the back of the sofa, not quite round her. His sister Belinda was coming tomorrow. Husband. Two children. He was a Deputy Head Teacher. They lived twenty-odd miles away.

'They knew one another at school,' Moira said, and

indicated a wedding photograph on the dresser. Belinda, puffy taffeta sleeves and a floral doughnut on her head. Is that how it would be? Should be?

And if it was, why not? Olive had no answer to give. What she felt inside herself, an unreality, even a panic, was no answer. She glanced at Malcolm's hand, alongside her own shoulder. A clean hand. That was right. Clean.

As she crossed the landing to the bathroom, she heard 'Really nice girl' murmured from behind a door.

There were two bathrooms. No jumble of other people's toothbrushes and flannels.

'Really nice girl.'

There were books in her pleasant, quiet bedroom – good though not new novels, the Bible, *The Oxford Book of Verse*, a Roget's Thesaurus, a Complete Shakespeare. Some Enid Blyton school stories. 'Belinda Crowley' written in careful ink. *Anne of Green Gables. Rebecca of Sunnybrook Farm.*

She took *The Forsyte Saga* from the shelf and plunged into the family and their world at once.

Just after midnight, she heard a sound. Silence. Then a soft sound again. Her door handle turned.

'Hello?'

'I just . . . you know. Are you all right? Everything you need and – all that?'

He wore pale blue pyjamas and a navy dressing gown with red piping that looked new.

'It's all really – really nice. Thank you. I'm fine.'

He came into the room. Hesitated. Closed the door. She did not know what to say and so after a moment turned back to her book, but the words blurred on the page.

'It's a really nice room,' she said.

He looked at her. Why was he looking at her?

'Are you all right, Malcolm?' she asked, after several more moments.

He came over and climbed onto the small double bed and lay down and rolled on his side towards her.

Olive's mouth went dry. She could say nothing. Not 'What do you want?', not 'Go away' – anything she might have said that she really meant would have sounded impolite. And she was a guest.

'Put your book down. It's a heavy book.'

She did so, keeping her place first, carefully, with the ribbon marker.

There was silence. He reached over her and switched off the lamp.

'This is all right?' he said. 'This is OK? You're all right with this?'

She did not know. Not when he touched her body. Not when he tried to remove her nightdress and had to ask her to do it. Not when she smelled his familiar smell and felt his unfamiliar smoothness. Then she felt something . . . a small stirring of pleasure, even a shadow of excitement. Of wanting. Wanting more. Yes.

'You're all right, aren't you? You know what I mean . . . this is all right?'

She supposed he was asking whether she was happy to accept it. Liked him. She was unsure.

She did accept him and then felt a pain that astonished her and with it a sense of having her entire self known by another person, as it had never been. The pain went on for a short time, and then stopped, but the sense of pleasure and wanting disappeared and the feeling that she was no longer her own self and never would be again did not leave her for years.

How to look him in the face the next morning? But he was as before, as usual. Olive felt as if they could all see through her, that she was transparent and they knew.

Belinda. Nigel. Tim. Penny. Roast beef. Apple pie. Cheese. The children raced about in the garden. Nice children. Nice-looking. Could they see through her too? She knew that Belinda was appraising her and she did not want to be appraised. She did not want to be here. It rained and the children came pelting in. Belinda gave her mother some sort of meaningful look.

Olive picked up some plates and took them into the kitchen.

'Why have you come to lunch?' Penny had slipped in behind her, silent as a shadow.

'Because they very kindly asked me.'

'I see. Do you like them?'

'Do you mean your grandparents?'

'Everybody.'

'I do.'

'Have you got any children?'

'No. But if I do, I hope they'll be like you.'

'Why?'

'Because you're both so well behaved and you're both fun and I love the colour of your hair.'

'But Tim has brown eyes.'

'And you've got blue.'

'Blue eyes are best.'

She was not exceptionally pretty, but she had such spark. She seemed to quiver with life and energy. Beside Penny, her brother was dull. Nice. Well mannered. Dull.

The spark was everything.

Malcolm came in with more plates, Belinda with dishes.

'I'll get the rest,' Olive said.

'I'll help you. I want to stay talking to you,' Penny said. And took her hand and the spark and the life seemed to leap between them.

Olive looked round the front room where they had coffee and chocolates. A family. Malcolm had his arm along the back of the sofa again, not quite touching her.

Family.

She felt as if she were itching all over, with frustration, irritation and with the need to leave, now. Nice people. A family.

She never wanted to see any of them again.

8

'ARE YOU happy, Olive? You often look so serious.'
'Do I? I'm sorry.'

'Solemn. Yes, solemn is better. You were a solemn
little girl of course.'

Was she? She did not remember feeling solemn.
She had played, as small girls play, raced about the
garden with friends, like Belinda's children, laughed
at silly jokes. She remembered one. She and Monica
Peel had told it to one another over and over
again.

'What did the earwig say when it fell off the wall?'
''Ere-we-go.'

They had shrieked with laughter every, every time,
so how could her father say that she had been
solemn?

* * *

Her first year was over and she was home in Leamington for the long vacation. She went to the library for Victorian novels, for they were to have their time in the sun next term, and at the library, she saw a notice advertising a vacancy for holiday relief staff.

'*Strictly not a permanent post. Enthusiasm and a tidy mind important. No experience necessary as training will be given.*'

'I remember you, Olive, of course I do. I can't think of anyone I would rather have to work here.'

Biddy French had been Librarian for as long as Olive could remember. Very short hair, in a bristle cut, which had always been white, above a soft, young-looking face. Eyes that looked and looked into Olive's own, as if searching for something there.

She learned everything quickly, because she had often observed it, and because she was interested, deft, well organised. The library suited her. It was quiet even when busy, with a satisfying peacefulness when it was not. She had plenty to do but was never rushed. It would not have been a stimulating enough job for her permanently but it was a delightful way of spending that warm, sunlit summer and earning money.

Malcolm wrote, friendly, slightly awkward letters,

words not being his forte. But he tried, describing, as carefully as in a school essay, the Italian resort where he had been with a friend's family, and giving news of his own, and asking after her, wanting to know what she was 'up to'. A couple of postcards came too, weeks after his return. One of them was also signed by Moira Crowley.

Olive wrote short replies, friendly, not intimate, and did not post any of them. She decided that, when her second year began, she would not see him again and so she tried to shut everything else about him out of her mind. It was not difficult. He had not made a strong mark.

It was hot for weeks. The grass on the verges and across the town parks turned yellow-brown. Trees shed their leaves early. The outdoor swimming pool was crowded every day with splashing, shrieking children. But in the library they kept the blinds pulled down, so that the rooms were cool and shady. People took refuge there. Old men stayed all day reading the newspapers and Biddy kept an eye but tolerated them.

On Fridays they stayed open until nine o'clock. Olive was stacking the last returned books onto a trolley ready to be shelved in the morning, Biddy was seeing out two last borrowers before locking and bolting the main doors. Staff came and went via a side exit.

Olive straightened her back and stretched.

'Are you in pain?'

Biddy was standing behind her.

'Not really, it's just bending over the trolley – things are never at the right height. I suppose they can't be, for everyone.'

She felt Biddy's hands on her, massaging her neck and shoulder muscles.

'Feel how knotted up you are! You must keep moving and stretching every so often.'

She kneaded her back. Olive felt the tension loosen, even while the pressure of Biddy's hands was making her muscles burn.

She did not want this. She wanted to pull away but was not sure how.

'Thank you, that's better.' She twisted slightly. 'I'm fine now, really.'

Biddy's hands went still but she did not take them away.

'Would you like a drink?'

'Oh . . .'

'Do you smoke?'

'No. No, thank you. I do have to get home.'

'One drink though, surely . . . nothing serious but I do have a bottle of rather good sherry. I don't suppose you're a whisky girl.'

Olive shivered.

She liked Biddy French. She enjoyed working with her. She was pleasant and fair-minded, she ran everything smoothly, she was popular with the borrowers and put her staff's welfare before her own. If there was an unpopular slot on the rota, Biddy would take it herself. If someone had to work after-hours, Biddy would.

Yet from the beginning, Olive had felt uncomfortable around her and was confused as to why, but the way Biddy looked at her sometimes made her feel awkward and she would try to get away to the other side of the library. Why? What could happen? Biddy French wasn't dangerous. She wouldn't . . . what? Wouldn't what?

Now, she felt the hands on her back and shoulders and neck, kneading again, smoothing, feeling, and some obscure part of Olive had, even without her realising, wanted it to continue. In a moment of panic, she fled to the thought of Malcolm. Malcolm in her bed. Malcolm's closeness and smoothness and it reassured her at once, it felt right, now that she remembered it, right in retrospect as it had not felt right when it had been happening. Not right. No, but not wrong. Not out of place, not unnatural, as Biddy French's hands on her back had felt.

'No, thank you but I really have to get home.'

She saw Biddy's face for a split second, shadowed

with hurt and disappointment, before she turned briskly, waving a dismissive hand.

Olive hesitated and then half ran towards the door.

9

D REAMS.
    Dreams?

She woke at three o'clock and again at half past five and then lay as the moon washed like a gentle tide over the carpet, the wall, her bedcover. Her.

The moment she had surfaced and before the moonlight, she remembered Biddy French and felt anxious and uneasy. Yet she had only been concerned and kind.

She had been something else. Olive knew that.

There were women. She knew that too. She had read things and been surprised but not shocked. Puzzled. Even amused. And then forgotten about it. It held no interest for her. She remembered that, just once, her mother had referred to women who shingled their hair and wore men's dinner jackets and ties. She had looked up from a photograph in an old magazine, of a tall, slender woman with very dark eyes and closely smoothed-down shingled hair, with a cigarette in a holder. She looked elegant.

'But she's in a play, isn't she?' Olive had said. 'She's acting.'

Evelyn's face had set in an expression Olive had never seen before.

Until she was sixteen she had had long hair, tied back for school, put up for going out, or occasionally left loose, but it had come to irritate her, washing and drying it took too long, and so she had had it cut, and when short, it waved a little. Her mother's was long and coiled at her neck, or plaited on top of her head, and at first she had regretted the loss of her daughter's long, silky hair, knowing but not saying that men found long hair more attractive. But Olive had chosen, and besides, there had been no shingling, just a smooth bob to her chin. Women had short hair now, curly, or straight, often permed. It meant nothing. None of them, that Olive had ever seen, wore men's formal shirts and trousers and dinner jackets, except on stage, in plays.

She should go to work as if nothing had happened.
Nothing had happened.

Had it?

She was on the middle-of-the-day rota. Biddy would be there. So would Sandra. But it was not a late opening.

She wanted to call in and say that she was unwell. But she was not and she knew that Biddy would realise.

Go. Go in and face her and carry on as usual. Keep away from her if she was embarrassed.

'Do you feel all right, Livi? You look a bit washed out.'

Her father always made breakfast – nothing cooked, but cereal and toast and tea and jam or honey and sometimes fruit. He laid the table, set everything out. They shared jobs, he did not expect Olive to wait on him.

'I do things for myself when you're away, after all.'

Now, he looked across at her, though not with more than a fleeting concern.

'I just woke up too early.'

'Not like you.'

'No.'

There was a letter from Moira Crowley. Malcolm would be twenty-one in October. They were giving a large dinner party – hotel, friends, drinks, five courses, and a family lunch the next day. Of course she would be invited, this was just to let her know well ahead of the date, and of course she would stay.

'*Yours affectionately,*
Moira.'

Of course.

Of course.

She showed the letter to her father. He put on his glasses.

'And will you want to go? They seem very nice people but this is your life not mine ... That is a friendly letter. But you don't have to accept, you know. One rarely *has* to accept.'

'I know. Of course.'

She realised that her father understood her better than she had known, and for a second, she wanted to tell him about Biddy French. He would have listened and understood and given sane advice if she had asked him for it. Far better tell him, as she could never have told Evelyn. She did not hesitate because of anything at all that he might think or say, but because of what she herself felt, her own uncertainty and embarrassment, which she had not yet made any sense of.

She replied accepting Moira's invitation, and then wrote a second letter, addressed to 'The Librarian', resigning from her temporary job 'because of unforeseen circumstances'. Biddy would have every right to withhold two weeks of her wages, or even insist on her finishing her time there.

But Olive knew that she would not.

10

S HE HAD slept with Malcolm. Or Malcolm had slept
with her. Because although she had not rejected or
resisted, somehow it felt as if it had been only his doing.
She was naive, she was innocent. But not ignorant. Her
mother had never once talked to her about any of it,
and so, along with some facts, she had also picked up
the old wives' tales everyone seemed to believe.

'You can't get pregnant the first time.' She believed
that, and by now, she had proved it, at least as far
as she herself was concerned. But she had accepted
the invitation to Malcolm's birthday celebrations
and he would surely expect her to sleep with him
again. Perhaps his parents had guessed or at least
suspected. Perhaps not.

But it would no longer be the first time. Presumably she would now be at risk.

'You were bloody lucky, ask me,' Margaret Reid said.

They were lying propped up on their elbows on a grassy bank in the park, eating ice-cream cornets. In the playground nearby, children were sliding, swinging, spinning round.

'And you are quite sure?'

'Of course I am, it was weeks ago.'

'Bloody lucky.'

'So . . . so what should I do?'

'You?' Margaret lay on her back and watched an aeroplane trail uncoil itself slowly across the sky.

She was the only person Olive could ask. There would probably have been a book in the library, if she had dared to go there. She wanted to tell Margaret about Biddy French too but that would be impossible. What was there to tell? If she thought about it, the whole incident evaporated and disappeared, like the plane smoke. Telling about Malcolm had been surprisingly straightforward.

Margaret's eyes were closed and she was swivelling a grass stalk between her front teeth.

'Marg?'

'You?' she mumbled round the stalk. 'You do nothing. That's his responsibility and he should know that and if he doesn't then you have to tell him, Oli.'

* * *

Olive rehearsed it in her head for the next few days, whispering, taking walks and muttering the dialogue aloud. Have you ... will you ... shouldn't you ... wait ...

It was impossible. But perhaps he ...

No. If he hadn't thought of it the first time, why would he think of it now? He might not know, she had said to Margaret, and got a sideways look. The stalk still went to and fro in her mouth.

'Maybe I should ... I could go and see the doctor.'

Dr Bonney, who had known her since she was two, who had vaccinated her and listened to her bronchitis and soldered her warts and stitched her upper lip after a dog had bitten her.

Of course not.

No.

She just wanted to leave it. Trust to luck.

Yes, and perhaps Malcolm wouldn't ...

But he would.

'I can't go to Dr Bonney, I just can't.'

'There's that new surgery – the Welmer Health Centre. I don't know anything about it, mind you.'

It was a bus ride away, and served the expanding Welmer estate and she felt an inexplicable sense of relief when she saw it, a single-storey building with a red-tiled roof. Nobody would know her in the neat rows. Briar Close. Bracken Close. Gorse Avenue. Cherry Crescent. New, hopeful little houses, the paint on the front doors still bright, grass linking them together. No front gates. No walls. No high hedges. It would be filling up with couples, families. Cats. The bareness took her aback. There were no trees. But things would soon grow – even the saplings, sleeved in plastic. They would grow. The health centre had windows to the ground and rows of chairs joined together, uphol-stered in tweed. Red. Blue. Red. Blue. Red. Blue. Red. Abstract murals, red and blue but also yellow. It smelled of newness.

The glass doors closed by themselves.

'I'd like to see a doctor. Please.'

'Appointment day or open surgery?'

'I don't . . .'

'We're trying out a new system . . . You can either come and wait, Mondays, Tuesdays and Thursdays, or make an appointment for Wednesday or Friday.' It was Monday.

'I'll wait.'

'Dr Freeman and Dr Singh are on this morning. Are you registered with either of them?'

'No.'

'With Dr Ferney or Dr Mansell then.'

She had very shiny very bright pink nails and very shiny matching lipstick. Olive thought she would try painting her nails for the birthday weekend.

'So, which doctor is it?' Her eyes looked past Olive, who felt a queue lengthening behind her.

'I'm not . . . I haven't joined this surgery. Yet.'

She sighed, though it was a sigh more implied than audible.

'Right. Your name and address?'

Olive lowered her voice, afraid the whole queue and the whole packed waiting room ahead would hear. Hear and know. Hear and repeat.

'Where is that?'

A bright pink nail tapped a street map on the wall.

'Oh – here, is it?'

'Yes.'

'We don't cover that part of the town. You can see the red circle? Only streets inside that. You want Dr Bonney's surgery. Belvedere Road.'

As she turned away, she caught sight of the notice-board. The notice. She had no pen or paper, but in any case, there would have been embarrassment in writing down the details with the room full of people watching. She stared at information about hearing loss while memorising the address and phone number on the notice above.

* * *

An hour later, she leaned against a wall, the sun glaring in her eyes, which gave her a public excuse for crying. It was hot again. The summer was stale.

They had been so nice to her. Kindly, the word seemed to be. It had been unexpected. The tears had already pricked the back of her eyes as the nurse, the kindly nurse at the Family Planning Clinic, had told her that she could not have an appointment. Three other women were waiting, much older than Olive. One turned the pages of a magazine she was not actually reading, the others just sat, staring ahead. Another woman came out of a door marked Room 3. A buzzer sounded.

'Mrs Derricks?'

The magazine woman had got up.

Perhaps no one had been listening.

'I'm afraid we can only see married women. Or those about to be married, if they have evidence of a wedding date. It's just the rule. Do you understand? We're very strictly regulated. I'm so sorry. But when you . . .'

She felt angry now, leaning against the hot brick wall. Angry with them, angry with herself. She should have checked first, should have thought. She could have thought. Checked. Someone would have . . .

How strange that it should be humiliating to be unmarried.

11

O n t h e Friday afternoon, the day before
Malcolm's birthday, Belinda and Nigel's
daughter Penny was killed, running out from behind
an ice-cream van into the path of a lorry. Belinda,
waiting on the opposite side of the road, talking to
another child's mother, saw everything. Saw. Shouted
a warning. Saw. Heard. Screamed.

As it was happening, Olive was on the train and
almost at her station, taking her bag down from the
rack, looking out for Malcolm, who was not there
and did not come, and so she got a taxi and arrived
in the middle of the agony and chaos and police presence and disbelief.

'I'll go back. I shouldn't be here.'

There would be a train home in an hour. But
Malcolm, in the kitchen making tea, because that was

all there was to do, clung to her. His face seemed to have sunken in, like a cliff after a landslip. He looked at her out of desperate, baffled eyes. Help me.

And then the house emptied, cars drove away, without anyone having come near them, and then the place was as still as death. He took Olive's bag upstairs. Came down. Filled the kettle again and lit the gas and every separate sound was a drumbeat falling into the silence. They sat at the kitchen table next to one another and Olive put her hand out and he took it and clutched it. She had only known one death, and that had been untimely and shocking, but not like this. There were neither words nor thoughts and not yet even feelings for this. She saw Penny, running in from the rain, laughing, and turned her mind away from the image.

They came back in the early evening, and still no one knew what to say. Peter. Moira. Malcolm. Olive. Someone poured drinks. Gin. Sherry. Olive cut sandwiches which no one ate, but they all drank again.

Naturally the dinner and the lunch were cancelled, but people telephoned. A neighbour left flowers fresh-cut from her garden. Another left a cake. Peter switched on the television and switched it off again.

'You're a dear girl,' Moira said, as they washed up

cups and glasses later. 'So good of you to stay. So good.'

'I had to. I couldn't have gone home. Of course I couldn't.'

And that was the truth.

Moira Crowley came over and put her arms round Olive and wept.

What should she say? What did people say? What did they do?

She could say nothing. Do nothing. Endure.

Malcolm came to her as soon as they had all gone upstairs and cried, lying pressed against her, clutching her again, and Olive caught his tears and held his head to her breast to comfort him, in spite of a feeling, deeply buried, that she should not do this, because it was the wrong way of things and somehow hurtful to him, and unfair. But she pushed those thoughts away and all she could do after that was let him find some closeness and comfort from her.

12

S HE WAS in the middle of an essay comparing
two villains in novels by Trollope and George
Eliot.

The Victorians were more sinewy with stronger
backbones than she had expected, having read little
of them beyond *Jane Eyre*, but they still seemed
over-rich and diffuse, their poetry even more than
their prose, when she preferred rich but spare. Her
tutor had told her that she was too devoted to form
at the expense of content, and asked why she was
afraid of 'lavishness of expression'.

If she worked and did nothing but work, she could
keep other thoughts at bay.

But the next morning, a letter came from Moira
Crowley.

We are all carrying on as best we can. We have to, for Belinda and Nigel's sake. But it is hard. Timothy is very quiet and withdrawn, and when Nigel tried to talk to him about his sister, he stuffed his fingers in his ears. Poor child.

Dear Olive, we hope you may be able to come and see us soon. We so love having you. Perhaps Malcolm will bring you one weekend before too long. You have been the greatest support to him. This is a time when our affections are tested and you have sailed through that test with flying colours.

But she had done little or nothing, of that she was sure. She had found it distressing and felt an intruder into their appalling shock and grief and pain. She set the letter down.

She liked them. There was nothing about any one of them that she could possibly dislike. But she was still an outsider, and wanted to remain so. She wanted to mean nothing to them.

Messages to say that Malcolm had rung were left in her pigeonhole, and when she was in and he called she pretended not to hear, and so he wrote to her, a rather formal, and yet raw, infinitely sad short letter, asking her to ring him, wanting to take her home with him in a fortnight's time.

She did not reply.

Several girls from school were married that year. The local paper ran photographs. Sally Redgrave wore a white trouser suit, which shocked the town and got her picture on the front page. Joan Curtis married a Spanish horse rider and wore a mantilla. Joan Loomis married a man she had first met when they were in their prams. The photograph showed them as babies, side by side, and then as a married couple in the church porch. Her father sent the cuttings to her. She stared at them, friends quite altered, astonished that only a short time ago they had been wearing navy-blue skirts and white shirts, gold-and-navy-striped ties, and house and games captain and prefect badges. They had all been looking forward to a future of training, careers, new places, new horizons. Doors seemed to have closed on them all now. But they probably wanted them closed. None of them looked unhappy or unwilling.

Margaret Reid sent a piece of crumbling wedding cake in a paper-lace-lined box and the smell of dried fruit and sherry puffed out as Olive lifted the lid.

She felt that she had escaped from something but wondered if freedom was better, when uncertainty and the unknown were its boundaries.

Her tutor for the Victorian novel had written books about it, whose titles appeared regularly in footnotes and bibliographies. He was a generally mild but occasionally excitable man who, if the subject stirred him, or an essay was laden with errors or opinions at odds with the text, would seem to explode and wave his arms about. Then he would subside and sit, eyes half closed, listening, still as a cat waiting to pounce.

She feared ridicule for her essay, though she had come to appreciate George Eliot and Trollope for previously unsuspected depths and for their occasional moral abrasiveness. When she had finished reading it aloud there was a silence, from her three fellow students and from the tutor, who she thought had barely been listening.

But after a moment, he said, 'Miss Piper, would you be so kind as to read your final paragraph – the summing-up?'

She read it.

'Yes,' he said. 'You have set out your stall and your conclusion is well argued . . . you have sold it to me. Let me hear what the others have to say, but for me, that is a very fine piece of work.'

She had been given praise and high marks before, for the work on her poets, but those essays had been a labour of love. This had been hard work and represented some sort of conversion. She could do more than she had expected, and she smiled to herself, going up the old staircase that curved at the top and curved again, where it led to the new wing and the second-year rooms. She was reminded of being four or five years old, when suddenly words in the newspaper her father was reading had, by some magic, gone from meaningless hieroglyphics to something understood, as she had stared at them.

'Sun and rain,' she had read aloud. 'Sun and rain.'

And her father, on checking the page, had laughed and applauded and praised her and she had felt that there could be no greater joy in the world than this clear and visible transformation of nonsense into sense.

The following morning, she realised that she had missed her period for the second time.

13

ONLY THREE others got off the train, and they quickly disappeared, one into the only waiting taxi.

Olive went to the booking office. She had a full duffel bag and her purse. Nothing else. It felt cold.

'I wonder if you can help me?'

He said nothing.

'I've come here for . . . for a few days. I'm not sure. But I haven't booked anywhere to stay. Do you know a hotel or . . . well, somewhere that would be . . .'

Cheap? Quiet? Safe for a young woman on her own?

'You by yourself?'

'Yes. But I'm meeting friends . . . tomorrow. Or maybe the day after.'

He looked at her, as if he could see through her to her soul. Certainly he could see that she was lying.

She could hear the sea. The wind was banging a gate.

'The Seagull. They're on the top terrace. B&B. If you can run to a hotel you'd be best off at the Belmont. End of Shore Street, turn left onto the front. You can get a nice room looking over the sea, I hear – if you'd want that.'

'Would they have a vacancy, do you think?'

'This time of year? They'll bite your hand off. I could ring and ask for you?'

There was no other taxi, and in any case, it was a short walk, he said. For the first stretch, street lights and those from a few houses helped her make her way. Plenty of the cottages were dark. Holidays were over. Then the lights petered out and she found her way by the sound of the sea.

On the open front the wind blew hard into her face, whipped up her hair, and the tide rushed in on the other side of the wall.

The Belmont Hotel was at the far end. She hesitated in the doorway, caught in a moment of panic, wondering how she came to be here. Getting away, anywhere, anywhere, had been her only need. She had gone to a station, looked up at the departures board and bought a ticket and got on a train, and for four and a half hours, she had slept, huddled in her coat. The train was full for a while but then emptied out at one station and the next, and then it was two hours on her own in the carriage. She had tried to blank out all thought. She had brought books, but in the end she just slept and after sleep went into a waking trance as they juddered through the dark.

The hotel was silent and smelled of beer and polish but they had a room at the front, and as they were 'quite quiet', the woman said, she could have a small double for the single rate. They went up two flights and everything was the colour of port wine and the shades on the wall lamps were pink. But the room was pleasant and not pink – the curtains were a dusty gold. She could hear the roar of the sea.

'Will you want supper? It's served from seven until eight but most people come early.'

She was hungry. She had only eaten a bar of chocolate from a vending machine on the station platform.

'Do you think . . . would it be possible for me to have a cup of tea?'

'Yes, but you'll have to come down for it – we don't do room service.'

*   *   *

She washed her hands and face. Brushed her hair and tied it back. Looked in the mirror and did not know herself. Unpacked her bag and took *Bleak House* downstairs. Her feet made no sound on the port-wine carpet. A door swung open with the wind behind it, and bumped shut again, but in that moment, let in not just the boom but the smell of the sea.

She hesitated at the door marked BAR, heard loud male laughter, and turned away, into LOUNGE.

One quiet couple, one woman alone.

She chose a seat near the fire which was made not of real but of electric coals. Port-wine velvet curtains were drawn against the night.

She opened *Bleak House.* She could dispense with other novels by Dickens, but never this.

'Fog up the river . . . fog down the river . . .'

At the end of the sentence, she jumped as if someone had spoken to her suddenly. But the room was quiet apart from the occasional low murmuring of the couple to one another and the voice she had heard was in her own head.

'You are going to have a baby. You are going to have a baby . . . You are . . . You . . .'

And then she saw it written up in front of her mind's eye.

'You are going to have a baby . . .'

'Fog up the river . . . fog down the river . . .'

'You are going to have a baby . . .' The writing scrolled down slowly like the credits at the end of a film, the one and then the other.

'You are going to . . .'

A clock in the hall struck seven and at once the quiet couple and the woman alone got up, and Olive got up too, and followed them into the hall, which smelled of onion soup.

Dining Room.

Pink lamps. Pink cloths. Port-wine carpet. But it was warm and not too large. One table was already occupied. The quiet couple sat down, then the woman alone. She chose the table adjacent to Olive's.

'You are going to have a baby,' the menu read. A small piece of paper with typed words.

'You are . . .'

Eggs Mimosa
Or
Cream of Onion Soup
Or
Fruit Juice

Lamb Cutlets
Or
Cod and Chips

Or

Omelette

(Choice of Cheese or Mushroom)

Potatoes. Mashed or Chips

Seasonal Vegetables

A waitress appeared through the swing doors with a pint of beer on a tray, and as she passed, the yeasty smell reached her. She had always liked the smell of her father's bottled stout but this seemed very strong.

She did not feel sick but the fumes of this ale repelled her and she moved her chair a little.

'You're going to . . .'

She had brought her book.

'*Fog up the river . . . Fog down the river.*'

The food was not unlike the food in college. She felt self-conscious drinking soup alone. But it was good soup and why should she not be here by herself?

Why was she?

She could just as easily have ended up in Cardiff or Reading. Exmouth. York. Edinburgh. Anywhere.

She had written a note to her father, saying that she had come away from London for a few days to concentrate on the books she had to get through for reading week.

She would have to leave, of course, though she might manage to the end of this term. But they would not want a pregnant unmarried student remaining in college until the end of the year. She could not go home.

She could not tell Malcolm. Malcolm would panic and tell his parents and they would assume that he would marry her. They would want it. Welcome it. Penny's death had left a gap in their lives and hearts they would be desperate to fill.

Should she tell her father?

She knew that she could never get rid of a baby, even if she had had the least idea how anyone went about it. It had been her first certainty. So, people would find out, inevitably. She would not have to tell them.

Treacle Sponge and Custard
Or
Sherry Trifle
Or
Cheese and Biscuits

Tea or Coffee

She did not eat very much and she was first back to the lounge beside the electric coals, before the others.

She could ask Margaret Reid – now Margaret Don-
ner. Or even Mary. They had always had answers and
information, between them.

But not about this.

'*Fog up the river . . .*'

Presumably she ought to see a doctor before long.
Just not Dr Bonney.

So, here then. She could say that she was moving
to live in this town. Find the address of a house to
rent. No one would know her.

The door opened on the quiet couple, with the
woman alone behind them and she glanced at Olive,
glanced again, and came to sit near her. Olive got up.

'Please, have this chair. It's the warmest place. I'm
going to my room now.'

'I wouldn't dream of it, I'm fine here. Aren't you
staying for coffee? Do stay. It's better coffee than you
might expect.'

Olive subsided into her chair, not knowing how to
refuse without seeming rude. And why would she
want to refuse? But she did not want to give off the
smell of loneliness. The coffee came in a metal pot
with a scalding hot handle and cups which were fluted
round the rim.

'You're rather young to be holidaying alone.'

'I'm not . . . I mean, it isn't a holiday.'

73

'Oh?'

'I've just come for a few days of quiet – to work.'

Without saying anything, the woman seemed to be urging her on, her face full of interest. Apparent interest?

'I'm doing a degree. In London.'

The bright, interested look was like make-up, not altogether convincingly applied.

'It's reading week.'

She had not meant to stammer on and the woman waited, but Olive drank her coffee, keeping the cup to her lips after she had swallowed and her eyes on the electric coals.

The door closed on the quiet couple.

'How long are you staying then?'

The woman had a pleasant, soft voice, and fair hair fading to grey, hair that stood round her head in a halo.

'How old are you?'

It seemed a rude question, even before the woman had given her name and asked for Olive's, but she did not apologise, just waited for a reply.

'Twenty-three,' she lied.

'Will you have a liqueur with me? We can order what we want from the bar and they'll bring it with more coffee.'

'No,' Olive said, standing up. 'Thank you but I need to get some work done now.'

'Oh, surely not! It's after nine o'clock.'

'All the same. And I have to ring my fiancé.'

'Really?'

She doesn't believe me. The way she looked at me through narrowed eyes.

She doesn't believe me. What does it matter?

Olive turned at the door. 'His name's Malcolm,' she said. 'It was nice to meet you.' She went, without seeing the woman's expression.

Why had she done that? What had worried her?

She leaned against the door of her room, as if afraid someone might try to open it.

Why had she said that? My fiancé. Malcolm.

The woman had tried to be friendly. She was lonely, that much was obvious. There had just been . . . what?

She went to run a bath and the noise of the water splashing drowned out her thoughts and the woman evaporated into the steam.

She lay down and looked at her stomach. Touched it. Her own body was strange and alien to her. She looked the same but she was no longer her own self, the self she had lived in intimacy with since birth. She was no longer that person.

She turned on the taps again and let them run

until the water had covered her almost to her neck.

The sea was turning over and over within itself moodily, but there was no gale this morning and no waves crashing against the wall.

She would not have gone into breakfast. She wanted to find a telephone directory in the booth in the hall, but as she walked across, the quiet couple were just ahead and the man held the door, smiling at Olive, and so she had to go in. The dining room looked shabbier in the morning light, without the gold curtains and the pink shades. She asked for tea and toast.

'Nothing cooked? Nice bacon today.'

She shook her head and opened *Bleak House*.

'It's quite ordinary bacon,' the woman alone said, 'actually.' From the adjacent table.

Olive smiled without looking at her. Beyond the bay windows, a boy on a bicycle went past slowly, making hard work of the pedalling. The windows had a fine gauze over the glass which looked like dirt but she thought must be sea spray.

Her pot of tea came, and the toast cut into crust-less triangles.

'And how was the fiancé? Malcolm?'

She should have been wearing a ring, of course.

That is what people did when they were engaged to be married. She nodded and concentrated on buttering toast.

She had no idea how much money she had in cash. Would the hotel accept her cheque? Perhaps she ought to ring her father.

'You're not in any trouble, I hope.'

The woman alone sounded amused. What did she think, that Olive was a prisoner on the run? But she was right. 'In trouble.'

'No.'

'Good.'

Knives scratched plates and the kitchen door swung open, wafting in the smell of frying.

Her father would worry but he would send money. That was the easy part.

'Do you have the address of a local doctor please?' she asked the woman at the front desk.

'Oh dear – aren't you feeling very well, Miss Piper?'

'No – yes ... I'm all right ... I just ...'

'No, no, none of my business ... so long as it's nothing serious.'

Nothing serious.

Nothing serious?

The woman handed her a slip of paper.

Drs Marshall and Tait
30 Cliff Road
Phone 7713

'The phone box is there but you can just go. Surgery's every morning from nine till half eleven.'

The cliff path was steep, and halfway up, she felt giddy and had to sit on a wall. When she got there, she waited an hour.

Dr Tait. He wore a tweed jacket and a pipe smouldered in an ashtray on his desk. The smell nauseated her.

'I think I may be . . . I think I'm pregnant.'

'What makes you think so?'

'I've missed two periods.'

'Doesn't necessarily follow of course but if you're usually regular . . .'

'Yes.'

'Anything else? Nausea? Tender breasts?'

'Not really.'

'So, you had unprotected intercourse? Or was this what is euphemistically called "an accident"?'

'No . . . not . . . not really.'

'And you're how old?'

'Twenty-seven.' She did not know why she lied.

Perhaps she wanted to seem mature. But in that case . . .

'Not a teenager then. So why didn't you take precautions? You seem an intelligent young woman.'

'In the end . . . I mean . . . He . . .'

'That's right, blame the young man. But you're the one left holding the baby, you're the one who should have been responsible. Unless you were raped. I take it you weren't raped?'

Why did he 'take it'? She felt angry but there was nothing she could say other than 'No'.

'All right . . . so, what do you want me to do exactly?'

Olive did not know what to answer.

He sighed. 'There's no point in sending away a sample for a test – too early. Wait until you've missed period three and then come back – you never know, you might not.'

'Is . . .'

'Is?'

'What will happen to me?'

'Well, you'll have a baby, my girl, that's what will happen. Do you have family?'

'My father . . . my mother's dead. I'm an only one.'

'Not ideal then. And what does your father say?'

'I haven't told him.'

He sighed again but then leaned forward. 'Now listen, my dear . . . whatever you do or don't do, I beg you not to drink bottles of gin in hot baths, or jump off tables . . . never works. Or, more seriously, do not visit backstreet abortionists with knitting needles. And they still exist, they still exist. Don't do it. People die. Get married. Or not – it's up to him. Have the baby, and if you're still on your own, have it adopted, give it a better life from the start. Being an unmarried mother isn't any fun. Give someone what they long for and can't have. Understand?'

'Yes.'

'Good girl. You'll be fine. All right?'

'But the thing is . . . where would I go?'

'There's a pretty good cottage hospital here – good midwives and this practice looks after it.'

'No, I meant . . .'

He picked up his pipe and began to tamp down the tobacco with his forefinger. 'What did you mean?'

'Aren't there places for . . . ?'

'Homes for unmarried mothers and their babies? There are. Not here. But there's St Jude's in Tremear. They're good. From what I hear. You could go and look when you're quite sure. Now, my dear, I am guessing there's a full waiting room . . . Come and see me in a month's time.'

14

'I'M SORRY – I should have let you know. I didn't think.'

Home was home but she usually did let him know in advance, though not because she felt it was required of her.

Home was home.

Wasn't it?

'My dear girl, it's absolutely fine, how could it not be? It's just a surprise – a very nice one, of course, that goes without saying. Have you had any lunch?'

'It's five o'clock!'

'Is that all the luggage you've brought? Just the weekend then?'

Olive looked with surprise at the duffel bag beside her. Yes. All the luggage. It didn't seem to matter.

When she came down again from unpacking what

she had – *Bleak House* on her bedside table – her father was in the kitchen. She saw vegetables prepared and cut up in a pan of water, potatoes peeled.

'I need to talk to you.'

He looked hesitant, ruffled, as if she had caught him out in something.

'I'll put on the kettle.'

She wandered into the dining room. The best white cloth on the table. Glasses. Tumblers. The canteen of silver cutlery open.

Her father stood behind her. 'Come and have your tea. I can explain.'

It was not that she minded, or was upset, or hurt, not that she disapproved, not anything but a complete surprise.

Her name was Peggy Drummond, her father said. He had been taking the train to London and it was half an hour and then forty minutes late, and so, instead of remaining on the platform talking to the woman sitting next to him on the bench, he had suggested they go into the warm buffet. They had drunk coffee, and then gin and tonic, and, inevitably, got into the same compartment. At Paddington he had put her into a taxi and taken the one behind, as they were going in opposite directions.

He had thought very hard before looking her up

in the telephone directory when he had returned home.

'We have met two or three times – outings, you know – but then it occurred to me that I should test my cooking skills. I have been practising – I must say, I rather enjoy it.'

He had often looked troubled, or harassed, and now he did not. His face was the same – of course it was. And yet it was not.

'But you said there was something you wanted to tell me, Livi. You can talk while I separate some eggs.'

But separating and then whipping eggs meant him fussing about and making a noise and how could she possibly tell him now?

How could she possibly tell him?

Peggy Drummond arrived precisely at seven. By then, he had changed his shirt and tie, and was hovering between the kitchen and the hall. Olive watched him.

She was a large woman, well corseted, her hair blonde, puffed up and stiffened, like candyfloss on top of her head. A two-piece purple suit with a shiny finish.

She talked. She had been a buyer in a large city department store for twenty-three years. Two husbands, the first dead of heart failure, the second of liver cancer. No children.

'I never wanted them. I'm not maternal. I enjoy my job and I like a social life. I have always been keen on the theatre ... that was where I was going when I met Ralph.'

Two years earlier, she had opened a boutique.

'Nothing really for you, Olive, as a student, more for the middle-aged woman with a bit of pocket money. Still, if you do come in and see something you like, I'd always give you a bit of a discount.' She turned her head. 'She doesn't take after you, Ralph.' As if Olive was not there.

No. Nor her mother. Well, perhaps her mother a little – the high forehead and small mouth were from Evelyn.

He went in and out, carrying the best china vegetable dishes with an oven glove, seeming slightly in awe of Peggy Drummond. Or puzzled by her.

'This is wonderful, a man who cooks. I'm afraid I loathe cooking, I live on salads. Do you cook, Olive? No, I imagine you students are catered for?'

'I cook when I'm here.'

Another dish came in. Three vegetables, plus potatoes. Her father pulled off the cap on his bottle of stout, and at once the smell made Olive turn her head away, then get up quickly and leave. Her father continued to fiddle with lids and serving spoons. Peggy Drummond seemed not to notice.

She was not sick, only nauseous. She took some deep breaths, drank water, but when she returned to the table, felt no better. It was hard to force food down her throat. After another half-hour, she left them, to lie in bed on her side, which gradually eased the sickness and she fell asleep.

'My dear girl, how are you feeling? I've made tea and toast . . . do you feel up to an egg? Or grapefruit. I have rather taken to grapefruit lately.'

She drank four cups of tea and then, suddenly ravenous, ate two boiled eggs and a quantity of toast. Her father watched her, beaming encouragingly, as if she had been an invalid for weeks and was now showing faint signs of recovery.

'And Peggy now?' he said with a touching eagerness, looking at Olive for approval. For reassurance?

'Yes,' she said and filled her mouth with toast.

'She has been very . . . you see, I think she's good for me. I was growing old before my time, Livi. I didn't go out except to the Lodge. I was becoming a bit set in my ways.'

'Do you go out now? With Mrs Drummond?'

'She did ask you to call her Peggy.'

'Sorry. Do you go out much with her?'

'We do go to the theatre. Occasionally to the cinema but there isn't often much of appeal there. And – and we dance.'

Olive's spoon stopped halfway to her mouth.

'Peggy is quite an accomplished ballroom dancer.'

'But you can't dance.'

'You'd be surprised. I've rather taken to it.'

'Like grapefruit.'

But he only looked vague.

The post flopped through the letter box. Olive fetched it. There seemed little of interest other than what looked like an envelope containing tickets.

'But I'm sorry . . . you still haven't told me whatever it was.'

She did not want to tell him now.

Could she leave it?

Might she just never tell him?

'I hope it isn't a worry about your work?'

Unexpectedly, her father reached out and covered her hand with his.

'You do know, don't you, that your happiness comes before everything? If you don't achieve top marks, what does that matter? It doesn't, not to me. I am proud of you no matter what.'

And his warm, dry, familiar hand, comforting for as long as she could remember, pressed firmly, and at that moment she understood his love, and how he had never failed her, never reproached her, except for the very occasional chastisement for some offence when she was a child.

And so she told him.

He went very still. Something in his expression changed but she could not quite interpret it.

She had gone over every one of his possible responses, in her head, for days, had expected him to be, in turn, shocked, angry, accepting, delighted, emotional.

He did not look at her.

'This would have killed your mother,' he said. 'She would have been devastated. She could never have borne it.'

How did he know that?

Of course he knew and he was right, but how was that of any importance?

There was silence, before he shook himself, out of thoughts that seemed to have taken him miles away from her.

When he spoke again, his tone was quite different.

'So, I take it there is to be a wedding? Peggy will be delighted. Any excuse for a new outfit, it would seem.'

Peggy?

'No.'

'I beg your pardon?'

'No wedding. I don't want to marry Malcolm.'

'But whatever else can you do? Please, please, Livi, don't risk your health and ... please don't ... you know what I mean.'

'Get rid of it. I would never do that either.'

'So dangerous. So dangerous. And illegal too, of course.'

'Is it?'

'Have you spoken to the college? Might they hold your place until – until afterwards?'

'I haven't told them.'

'And Malcolm? Irresponsible he may be but he does have a right to a say in this.'

'I haven't told him.'

'Then you must. Write to him tonight.'

'No, I ...' She did not meet his eye.

'Promise me that you will write to him.'

'Yes.'

Olive got up. Everything she had vaguely hoped for from him had not come about, though what that was she could not have said. Understanding? Love?

'Are you angry?'

'Angry? No. I don't think I am angry. Only shocked. And very disappointed. Worried. I hardly know what else to say.'

'Perhaps Peggy will advise you,' she said, and went out of the room. As she shut the door, she glanced back. Her father sat, staring at the breakfast debris. And then he reached for his cup and she saw that his hand shook.

15

Dearest Olive

I do so hope that a letter from me at once will not prove unwelcome but of course Malcolm has told us his/your news, and although naturally somewhat startled at first, I confess that both Peter and I are really quite delighted. As you know only too well this has been such a bitterly hard time for us all and we could do with some joy. Naturally, no other child can ever replace our darling Penny – but I am sure neither of you would expect that. This new little life should not be burdened in advance with a weight of expectations. He – or she – must and will be separate and distinct and welcomed for its own sake.

Please come and stay here as soon as you possibly can so that we can talk about the wedding. We understand that you may well want to keep it very low-key under the circumstances, but we are allowed to anticipate a very happy day all the same. We are all so looking forward to welcoming you as Malcolm's wife into our family, dear Olive.

With love and best wishes to you,

Moira (Crowley)

PS We have not yet told Belinda and Nigel and will be guided by you as to when you think it appropriate for us to do so.

16

THE SUN shone. That helped. How many people understood what a difference the sun made on a day like this. Days of death and funerals. Days of despair. The sun made life bearable, hope real, a future possible.

She thought that if she had come back here in rain and under billowing skies and with a sullen, churning sea she might have stood on the clifftop with her toes just over the edge until she overbalanced and fell.

But the sun shone.

ST JUDE'S
Under the Auspices of
THE CHURCH OF ENGLAND
MORAL WELFARE

She fumbled for her purse and tried to open the taxi door at the same time. The driver was surly, unshaven and with dandruff on his jacket collar like soap flakes, and he had not spoken a word to her all the way. But as she got out, he told her to keep her money.

'You'll need that,' he said, 'one way or another.'

She had not been able to look round as it was so far away, so now, she stood in the drive, looking at the home for the first time, as the sun touched the grey walls , and one or two faces peered out of upper windows, and were sunlit too, and the creeper was thick and dark, luscious green.

St Jude's.

'How do you do, Miss Piper?'

The handshake was rasping. Dry skin. Hard bones. But the matron smiled, seemingly also warmed by the sun.

'In a few minutes you can go up to your room, but come in here first. We shall have a talk.'

Parents?
Age?
Education?
Father of the child?

*   *   *

'Such a pity. You could be looking at a bright future. Well, perhaps ... I am a firm believer in second chances, Miss Piper.'

Should she ask to be called Olive?

Previous pregnancies ?
General health?
Obstetric health?
Plans?

Plans?

Apparently almost all the girls had the baby adopted. A very few wanted to keep it. 'But that is a hard, hard road – a struggle, and you know, money has little to do with it.'

A cup of coffee was brought in, for the matron. Nothing for her.

'Do you have anything to ask me? Anything at all?'

She did not, but for some reason blurted out that her father was paying, and for baby items, and giving her an allowance.

'And will the baby's father want to visit? And if so, before or after the birth?'

She lied that he had no interest in doing so.

Malcolm had begged to visit, begged her to marry him, begged to bring Peter and Moira when the baby was born.

'No.'

The matron pressed a bell and a girl with dyed red hair and a heavy pregnancy beneath a smock, knocked and came in.

'Take Olive to Room 9, Elsie, thank you. Introduce her. Show her round.'

The staircase. She still remembered the staircase years later, as she remembered the staircase in the old building at college, wide, curving. Why the staircases?

'It's not so bad, you know,' the other girl said, stopping on the half-landing and putting her arm round Olive's shoulders. Olive could feel the baby between them.

'Six weeks to go,' she said. 'And you look as if you've more, so they'll give you some of the hard chores then – scrubbing and window cleaning. It's easier as you get near your time. I just clear the pots and wash up. And then you've so much stuff to get ready. It's amazing how the days go by.'

Room 9. The number was on the door.

It overlooked the back of the house. A yard. A service area. Two trees. But then a field, and beyond the field, the sea. It was not close but still clearly visible in its deep grey-blueness.

Forever after, she remembered that first sight of it, and remembered how the first sight of it had made her inexplicably happy. Lifted her heart.

'You're here then. I've been on my own in this room for ten days.'

A thin wisp of a girl with pale hair and small features. She had a neat round of a baby, like a football.

'I'm Kay.'

'Olive.'

'My gran was called Olive . . . that's nice. How old are you? How far along are you?'

In what she became used to thinking of as 'the world' Olive had never met anyone who asked so many questions as Kay, the sort people were brought up never to ask.

What did your parents say?

Will you give it a name or let them choose?

Did they send you here?

Where do you live?

Have you told the father? What's his name? Did you get caught the first time? Have you been sick?

They came like pattering feet, one after another, the questions, but she found that she did not mind, and answered them all and asked her own, too, though fewer, and so they settled into a sort of friendship, borne of the shared room and this place and their condition. Years later, without warning, the image of Kay would come to her mind, the thin body, pale hair. It was as if she were standing there, asking her questions, questions.

'Do you smoke? You can smoke in the common room or outside, not anywhere else, only everybody does, we lean out of the window.'

'I don't smoke.'

'Why not?'

'I suppose . . . my parents never did . . . I tried once. I wasn't really attracted to it.'

'That's good . . . if only you'd been attracted to cigarettes instead of men, we'd have had a lot less grief. All right, well, what do you want to know about this place? Matron's a snake. Watch out for Nurse Pitt and Nurse Flynn, they'll get you in trouble, they enjoy it . . . the others are mostly all right. The cooks are lovely even if the food's awful but it's all right on Sundays . . . visitors can come to tea on Sundays though not many do. My gran came once, the last time.'

The last time?

'Work's hard.'

'Where are the babies? Where are they born?'

'The annexe – that's the brick building on the far side. You don't see or hear anything. Once

97

you've gone into the annexe then you don't come back here.'

'What do you mean?'

'You stay there from when the baby's born. And it stays in the nursery with the others, except for feeding. But when the six weeks are up and it goes, you go as well.'

'Go where?'

'Well, wherever you're going. I mean home or . . . wherever. The place you came from.'

'Why six weeks?'

'You don't know anything, do you?' And the girl reached over and touched Olive's face gently. 'Babies can't be adopted before they're six weeks, so you have them till the people who are adopting them come and get them.'

'They can't make you have your baby adopted. No one can force you to give your baby away.'

'I don't suppose they can . . . not force you. Only you can't very well keep it, can you? Where would you go with it and think what people would say? You'd be even more ruined than you are already.'

Kay's baby was due before Olive's so there would be a new girl sharing Room 9.

Meanwhile, daily life took over, and daily life was work, plus tiredness, aching back and feet, stodgy food and permanent constipation, plus knitting and sewing everything the baby would need. It would wear the clothes she made, plus a second set, in a size larger, when it was taken by the adopters, at six weeks.

Six weeks.

She was bad at sewing, clumsy and impatient, but a decent knitter and knitting sent her into a pleasant, quiet, dreamlike state of calm. She felt her child kick and turn and found the idea of it, the thought of another person, male or female, sharing her body, an alien one and bewildering.

Kay's small round baby-ball grew a little but the rest of her remained stick-thin. Olive felt that her own body swelled everywhere. She felt ugly and cumbersome, her legs thick as tree trunks, her face fuller, her stomach spread all round. She dreamed that her mouth was full of baby. She was choking on it.

But they laughed. Laughed as they worked, meeting on the staircase they were sweeping or by the shelves they were dusting, or the floors they were scrubbing, laughed over the knitting and sewing and eating and going out for bitterly cold walks, and on the bus they were allowed to take into town on Saturdays, laughed in the shops and the cafés and sitting on the bench overlooking the sea with fish and chips in paper. Laughed.

There was always something to laugh about.

There were ten rooms. One was kept for girls in isolation because of sickness, or insolent behaviour. When Olive arrived, there were twelve girls, who went down to nine, ten, then back to twelve.

Kay woke her up in the middle of one night, gasping, so that at first Olive thought she was in pain and heaved herself out of bed, to go and ring the bell on the landing.

'Go back to sleep,' Kay said. 'I'm only crying.'

'What is it? Are you sure you're not having pains?'

'I'm all right.'

She sat on Kay's bed and reached out for her hand. A gale was blowing off the sea, rattling the windows. Kay huddled down in her blankets.

'You can tell me anything.'

'No. I can't.'

'All right. If it's private . . .'

'Yes. That's what it is. It's private.'

Olive bent over and kissed Kay's cheek. It was cool. Soft. Like a child's.

'Thanks,' Kay said, and turned over. 'You're the best. Last time, I . . .'

'What? What do you mean, "last time"?'

Kay hunched herself up as well as she could

'I've been here before, haven't I? So that's it. Twice is very bad and there's no third chance.'

'Oh, Kay . . . why?'

But she did not answer.

'Did that baby go for adoption?'

She could barely hear the answer. 'Yes.'

'Poor you. Poor Kay.'

Kay lifted up the bedclothes. 'Come in.'

'No, we've got to sleep.'

But Kay waited and so Olive lay down beside her, and put her arms round her, and her baby pushed and kicked against Kay's back, and, comforted, they went to sleep, and did not stir until the morning.

Kay was on washing-up chores, Olive cleaning bathrooms, so they did not meet all morning and when the dinner gong sounded Kay did not come to the dining room.

Olive slipped out, leaving most of her blancmange, saying she needed to fetch her sewing scissors, but Kay was not there. The bed had been made carefully, the sheets drawn tight. At two o'clock, someone came into the sewing room and said that Kay had gone into the annexe. There was no other word. The day trailed on until supper and recreation time and then bed and Olive went up to the room alone, and lay reading.

Fog up the river . . .

*   *   *

101

The gale was still blowing. She lay listening to it, wondering what was happening to Kay. What did happen? She knew little beyond the biological facts. She had expected to be given information, even just things to read, but there was nothing. The birth of the babies was a secret ritual that went on behind closed doors and shaded windows in the other building.

At lunchtime next day, she asked.

'You're not meant to be told,' Nurse Goole said. But then softened. 'If I get any news, I'll try and let you know.'

Kay had a son. Nurse Goole leaned over Olive as she was clearing the supper tables, and whispered.

That Kay had had a slow and troublesome labour, with panic at the end and almost loss of the baby, was not told.

'When can I go and see her?'

Nurse Goole looked astonished. 'That is strictly not allowed.'

She did not explain. Perhaps Olive was expected to know the reason by some magical process, as she was expected to know everything else.

The annexe remained out of bounds and a new girl came to share Room 9, sullen, unfriendly Pat, who smoked cigarettes out of the window which let in cold

102

air and blew back the tobacco smell into the room. Olive turned on her side and read.

She never saw Kay again and the book became her closest friend.

But because she had nothing to lose, she started to ask questions and query rules, though always politely.

Why could no one visit girls in the annexe?

Why were they not given any preparation at all for the birth ahead?

Why was there no member of the staff they could talk to privately, about their fears and concerns? They could see a doctor or the Sister about physical worries. Why not this?

'Troublemaker, that one,' they said.

'Come in, Olive. Sit down. You haven't had any visitors?'

Not many of the girls did.

'I have had a letter from your father, enclosed with his monthly cheque, asking if he could come and see you. He sounded rather hurt. Is there any reason why you haven't sent me a visitor request? So many girls have no one, they've been ostracised by their families – or even have no one close. But you do and this will be a first grandchild, I think?'

'Yes.'

'So surely your father would like to meet it, before the adoption? To have a memory. It is permissible, you know.'

'Yes.'

'Think about it, Olive.'

Matron bent her head to her papers. Apparently, she was dismissed.

'Oh, and Olive . . .'

'Yes?'

'We don't have rules for rules' sake. I think you'll find there's a sound reason for all of them.'

'What is the reason for not preparing us for what will happen?'

'Your health is well looked after. You've had all the recommended checks.'

'That wasn't what I –'

'A word of advice. Sometimes it's best to meet things when you come to them – not cross your bridges. Not spend weeks imagining the worst.'

'But if –'

'That is also one of the reasons why we don't allow you to go and see the girls once they have had their babies . . . silly stories, horror tales . . . Try to tolerate us, Olive. We do have your best interests at heart, you know – yours and baby's.'

17

Her child was born on the day her father married Peggy Drummond, though Olive did not know anything about that until a week later, and by then, they, their marriage, whatever had happened, belonged to another time, almost another life, one to which she could barely relate.

There was a closed door and she had pushed and pushed against it, but it had not yielded to her, though in the end, after hours of struggling, she found that it opened quite easily, and she half fell through it, to find herself in another, quite unexpected, quite overwhelmingly beautiful place, knowing all things, understanding all things, but, principally, love. Perhaps she thought, as he lay still connected to her by the cord, perhaps this was what dying would be like.

Apparently her labour had been perfectly

straightforward and trouble-free, even on the short side, but as she had no template for it, she could only take their word.

She was exhausted and she could not sleep.

He weighed seven pounds four ounces and fed from her at once, greedily, born knowing how and suckling in a closed-in, concentrated place of his own, oblivious to everything else. To her.

When he was sated and they took him away to his cot among the other cots in the nursery, a corridor and a million miles away, she lay aching and sore and full of longing for him.

'What are you calling him?'

She had not realised that his name was hers to give, and said nothing.

'It's true that the adoptive parents can choose a different name of their own, Olive, but you're his birth mother, you register him. It's one thing you have.'

He was brought back to feed again in the early, dark hours, and when he latched on to her breast, she pulled back his flannel swaddling sheet and night dress carefully and examined every inch of him. A very little down of fair hair. Fine fair eyelashes. Mauve blue eyelids. Flat ears. Skin too soft for her finger to feel at all. Blush-pink nails. She cupped her hand round his head, leaned over and inhaled his smell, mingling with her own smell, seemingly still part of her. But separate now. Himself.

'James.'
  'Just "James"?'
  'Yes.'
  Mother's name. Olive May Piper.
  Father's name. Malcolm Crowley (Did Malcolm have any other names?)
  James. James Piper.
  She knew no one called James. Of course they could change it to the name they preferred.

Dearest Olive,
  Well, here we are, Mr and Mrs Piper! We're installed in a luxury suite, sea-facing, in Bournemouth and after a few days here heading for Jersey and Guernsey. Your father has never been to the Channel Isles, so it will be my pleasure to show him round, as I know them well.
  We had a lovely sunny day for our quiet wedding. Half a dozen friends, plus ourselves, for dinner at the Oak Rooms. I don't know if you know it? We were so sorry you weren't able to be with us but we look forward to seeing you soon.

All the best, my dear, from
Peggy (Piper née Drummond)

(Livi, and from me of course. Letters can be
received here until the 25th, then until the 7th
at the Belle Victoire, St Brelade's, Jersey, CI.
Then home, of course. I am sending you something via a separate envelope. I so hope all is
well with you. D.

A £100 cheque came the next day. Was he afraid to
tell the new Mrs Piper about it?

She stood by the window, cradling James. His eyes
were briefly open, though unfocused. Grey-blue eyes.
He did not look like anyone but himself. No one she
knew had those eyes. Then the lids came down.

'That boy – sleeps for his country. He never stirs,
you know, even when the rest of them are squeaking
and squawking. Whoever gets him will be a lucky
mum and dad.

Olive put her cheek to his head. To the down that
was so fine it was like spun air.

'One thing,' Kay had said, 'don't bond. Steel yourself against getting close to him, or it'll be the worse
for you. Don't let yourself love. I made that
mistake.'

How could that be done?

She came to know every atom of his long body, every expression on his face as they changed fleetingly, as when a cloud comes over the face of the moon. She knew his contented murmurings when he was milk-sated, knew the second before wind pained him and he drew up his knees, knew his crying from every other in the nursery, knew that he relaxed when she picked him up and he smelled her smell, and tensed as she put him down. She and he were woven together, threads going this way and that to make up a whole.

The word 'love' seemed inadequate to describe her feeling for him and she did not feel it only in her heart but in her gut and in the farthest reaches of her brain.

He smoothed out, lengthened, put on flesh and strength in his limbs, his eyes began to focus. His hands sometimes moved about in front of his face like fronds of weed under water and she saw how fiercely he concentrated on trying to make them out.

The pattern of his eating and sleeping fell into place, and the times when he was simply awake, now, awake and looking, were longer. She wanted to hold him to her all day and wrap him up close to her, skin to skin, at night, and when she was told to put him back in his nursery cot, and he cried, the milk came tingling into her breasts and spilled over, at the moment her own tears came with his.

The days merged. One week became two. Three. They ate in the small annexe dining room, the same food as in the main house, but with extra milk and orange juice, and a vitamin tablet beside every plate at breakfast. She was always hungry. She went twice on the Saturday-afternoon bus into town and was in a panic to leave him, in case she had some stupid accident which would take her from him. She bought biscuits and a boxed cake, chocolate, and at the last minute, before the next bus, a knitted cotton rabbit.

When she got back, he was asleep, and she put it in the cot, just touching his hand.

'I'm no good at this,' Noreen said, a girl Olive sometimes talked to when they were side by side changing nappies on the spread pieces of sheeting. 'I want her to be comfy and I know she isn't.'

Noreen's daughter, who had not been given a name, was tiny, with fists curled in upon themselves and spindles for legs. Olive looked at her son, robust, growing, flailing his arms as she washed him. His genitals seemed huge, out of proportion to the rest of him, but she was told that was usual. 'They grow into their bits,' a nurse had said.

Olive looked at them thinking that they were the only ugly thing about him, the scrotum's wrinkled, purplish skin, the bulbous testicles. She felt that she should not have been allowed to examine him so closely or touch what was so strange and personal.

Beside him, Noreen's baby was perfectly formed, with the delicate cleft tucked into her small body.

She had thought she would have a girl herself, but the moment he was born, it seemed right and inevitable that he should be he, and no other child would have been possible.

18

A TUESDAY afternoon and the windows were open onto the garden. After lunch and clearing up, five of them were sitting on the grass in the sun, Olive next to Noreen.

'She can wear that,' she said. Noreen held up the daisy chain. 'Not long enough yet.'

'Anyway, you can bet they'll take it off her again.'

'You wear it then.'

'I might just.'

Noreen seemed to think it was a day like any other. Almost seemed not to have registered the fact that sometime on this beautiful, warm afternoon, the people would arrive to take her baby away.

Olive picked daisies and split the stalks with her thumbnail neatly, and threaded the next flower through, and her focus was fiercely on this, how long she could make the chain, how carefully she could arrange it so that each daisy was exactly the same distance from the next.

Time had never speeded up like this before, days had never raced, never merged into one another seamlessly in just this way.

One baby had left. Noreen's went today. Wendy's would probably be next but no one could be sure. No one was told. It was thought to be better this way.

When her time came Olive did not know how she would bear it. She lay wide awake at night when he was feeding, drawing him even closer to her, as if she could somehow stop it happening. Keeping him back. She had even thought wildly of packing her bag and waiting until late, when no one would be in the nursery, and simply taking him, slipping out of the side door and running, running with him. He was hers, wasn't he? He belonged to her, not to St Jude's, not to the people who would come, thinking that he would be theirs. How could anyone stop her?

The idea came back to her now and seemed even more possible, even more right and the only solution. It was true that she had signed the papers, giving him up, but that had been just the day after his birth, when she had not known what was real and what false, and they had taken advantage of that. She had done it because she had not then understood what love was, or that there could be another way.

'No girl can manage this alone.'

'You want the best for your child, Olive, surely you do?'

'How would you face the world with an illegitimate baby? Ask yourself that. And how would he face it?'

She had signed the papers.

'They get paid,' one of the girls had said. 'People pay a lot of money for them.'

But surely that could not be true. Surely they would not be allowed to sell babies?

'I can hear them . . .'

Noreen turned her head to listen. There was the sound of a car coming slowly over the gravel at the front.

'Oh God, please God . . .'

Olive jumped up and took her hand. 'It might be anyone. But I'll come upstairs with you in case. You don't want to see them. I'll stay with you.'

They went up to her room because it was further from the nursery. Noreen sat on the bed, the pulse in her neck pounding. She was limp, like a doll someone had propped up against the pillow.

'Have some of this chocolate . . . and there's a cake I bought. I don't know if it's much of a cake though.'

'Would you go and look? Try if you can see them.

Please God they're nice, that they're a kind couple for her.'

'Listen, they'll be a little while. I can go in a bit. You look cold, Noreen.'

She was hunched up, her arms crossed over her chest, holding herself tightly. Her face was chalk-white. Olive sat down beside her and tried to make her take a small piece of the chocolate but she shook her head.

'I'd be sick.'

'All right. Doesn't matter.' She put her arms round the girl and held her and tears ran silently down Noreen's cheeks and fell onto the back of Olive's hand and on her arm. 'I'm sorry. I'm so sorry, Noreen. It's the hardest thing. It's the worst thing of all.'

'I'll be gone tomorrow, then. I'll be off from here.'

'Where will you go?'

'My sister said I could stay with her, just for a little while. She lives in County Cork. She has three of her own, which might help me. Or might not. And then – I don't know. I like Ireland. I might stay.'

'I never wanted a sister – or a brother either, I've always been happy just as myself. It never seemed to matter, but I can see now what a difference it could make. I'd like a sister now.'

'Do you think they're in the nursery, do you think they're looking at her?'

'I don't know. Try not to think of it.'

'What else can I think about?'

Olive was silent and just held her hand, gave her a handkerchief to wipe her face, and then they just sat, and it was all that filled her own mind too. She wanted to weep for Noreen. After a while, she realised that she had fallen asleep. She moved her carefully aside, laid her down and pulled the bedcover over her. Noreen stirred and turned half over, and the tears still slid down, but she did not wake.

The annexe was very quiet. The sun shone through the long, narrow windows, sending golden lances onto the stairs. Olive went slowly, cautiously down, stopping now and then to listen. But there was no one. There were no voices. She went to the window on the half-landing.

In the sunshine at the front of the house, two people were getting into a car and her heart jumped, as she saw them, and thought of Noreen, sleeping, and of what she had to wake up to, and felt her own tears prickle her eyes. She watched as the car moved slowly off. She caught a glimpse of a woman's hand, spread on a white shawl. The shape of someone at the wheel. She could not make out any more. The car went a little faster, but then stopped. Waited. Was something wrong? Were they changing their minds, coming back? But as she held her breath, watching and watching, a door opened along the corridor, and she retreated back. When she got to the top, she looked out again. The car had gone.

How to tell Noreen? What to tell her? How to explain that she had seen very little, but that little had been someone taking away her baby? She felt oddly responsible, as if she could have stopped them.

There was a burst of laughter from the kitchens. A radio played band music, behind someone's door. She would have a few minutes, because Noreen would still be asleep, and so she went down, and through the swing doors to the nursery. Mothers were not supposed to visit at random, pop in and out just when they liked, it unsettled the babies, they were told, and babies needed calm and routine. It upset the mothers, as well, getting into the habit of too much close contact when it would not be permanent. It was the quiet time of the afternoon. None of the nurses were about.

She went to the top of the room on the right, where James's cot had its place.

James's cot.

The space was vacant. His cot was not there, so who had moved it and why had they moved it? Perhaps something was wrong with him and they had taken him to isolation, or maybe he was just restless and being given a bottle of warm water to soothe him.

117

There were seven babies in the annexe at the moment. Seven cots. She counted six.

Seven. There should be seven. She went to each one and looked down at the swaddled, sleeping baby but none of them was hers.

The door opened.

'Olive? You should not be here. Who let you come in? I was just about to send for you.'

'What's wrong with him? Where is he?'

'He's gone, Olive.'

'What do you mean?' She could not take this in. It made no sense. 'How has he "gone"?'

'To his new home. They've taken him – his new mother and father. Your baby is adopted now, Olive. You have to try and forget him.

19

THE FLAT, which was officially Apartment 20, was on the top floor and reached by a slow lift. The entrance hall was silent, and bare, but in an attempt at decoration, two huge fan-shaped displays of orange and red artificial flowers and a pair of giant cactus plants, which might or might not be real, had been placed on ledges.

Numbers, and the names of occupants, were set into a row of small plates beside the lift. Apartment 20. Piper.

She had only brought her old duffel bag with a few overnight things.

'Livi!'

Her father was standing there as the lift doors opened and at once opened his arms to embrace her, a thing he had not done since her childhood.

'You look peaky – as your mother would have said. But well – how are you?'

'I'm fine. I never knew what peaky actually meant.'

He held on to her arm and his face was suffused with pleasure at seeing her. And love, she thought. Yes.

Peggy was in the sitting room, standing in front of the windows, which made up an entire wall. Grey sky beyond. Grey sea. Seagulls swooping and soaring.

'Olive! How nice.'

They did not know how to greet one another. As to shake hands seemed ridiculous, they did nothing.

Peggy's hair was the same blonde puffball. She wore another shiny two-piece, this time printed with flowers.

'Would you like some tea? I'll show you to your room first.'

Small, facing a green and an identical block to this. The flat smelled of new paint. New carpet. There were frilled curtains. Small cushions on a small bed.

Olive looked at herself in the dressing-table mirror – her old dressing table, which had reflected her face back to her over the years during which it had changed into her present, adult self.

Peaky. Was she? There were shadows beneath her eyes.

James, she said to herself. He was somewhere

unknown and lost to her. By now he would have for-gotten the sound of her voice, and her smell. She was lost to him, too.

James was not mentioned for the whole two days of her stay in the bright, over-cushioned flat. She wondered how her father stood the claustrophobia of its neatness, squareness, its lack of nooks and cran-nies, high ceilings. A garden. How he could bear to live pent up with Peggy every day, every night. She had never noticed Peggy's perfume before but in these small rooms it was heavy and cloying, and after a few hours, her own clothes and hair began to smell of it, or so it seemed.

She said she would like to go for a walk.

'I got used to being near the sea,' she said. 'I miss it.'

But they did not ask her anything about that, and so it went. If she said anything that touched upon where she had been and why, it was as though she had not spoken at all. She began to feel as if she did not exist.

Peggy would put her feet up, she said, so she went out with her father.

Blocks of flats were set all the way along the broad sea road with the occasional hotel between, once grand and imposing, now merely depressing. People walked along, people took the air, but without any other apparent purpose.

'Why did you come here?'

She looked sideways at her father but his expression was hidden.

'Oh, we thought we'd like to be somewhere new to us – have a change. And of course it's easier to manage. We didn't need all that space. Or the stairs.'

'You're not old.'

'Looking old age in the face, Livi.'

'That's rubbish. I loved our house.'

'So did I, my dear, so did I. Never think otherwise.'

'Then are you happy?'

'Of course. Yes, yes.'

Was he? She stopped to look at a ship on the horizon, and as she did so, it occurred to her that she had a choice – now, here. She could fret about whether her father had done the right thing, marrying again, coming to this town, confining his life to a small space, and whether he would be able to grow old here in some sort of contentment – and she was right, he was not old yet, only in his early sixties. Or she could simply leave him – them – to it, let them carry on with their life as they would have done if she had not existed. Trying to discover how happy he really was, if he had regrets, was pointless because his life was not hers. She had no need to concern herself.

She turned away from staring out at the ship.

'Dadda?' She surprised herself. How long was it since she had called him that? Ten, fifteen years?

He looked at her, and his expression was tender.

'You seem fine,' she said, taking her father's arm. 'It all seems fine. I'm glad you're happy.'

And so she chose. She felt a burden lift not from her shoulders but from her heart, so that it was free again and no one's but her own, after all.

They did not mention James. He had not existed for them. She did not feel disapproval or distress, but an emptiness. James would not know this grandfather.

The college had not allowed her back to finish her degree, and so she had applied elsewhere and found Keele, a new university anxious to attract good students. She wanted only to keep her head down, to work. Literature was her lifeline and her solace once again. The English tutors were modern with, to her, bizarre critical theories, but if she had confidence in nothing else, she had it in her own ability and power of independent thought, and these, allied to her enthusiasm, carried her through, past postmodernism and deconstructionism, past Marxist interpretation and the debunking of much of the literature that she held sacred.

She wrote the finals essays in a white heat. At the end of every exam her wrist burned and her neck muscles ached, and she leaned back in exhaustion, emptied of words, quite unable to judge her own performance, other than that she knew she had not been floundering, had written without pause.

The university was mixed and she had got on perfectly well with the rest of her year but made no close friendships, because she felt a hundred years older than them, and on the other side of a great divide. She had borne James and given him away and the experience separated her, and marked her out – though the marks were not visible to others.

20

S HE HAD answered two advertisements for teachers of English. Beechway College was four miles outside Tunbridge Wells and had a reputation for educating the daughters of the county well-to-do, and those of military and diplomatic families serving abroad. She faced a handsome building, surrounded by mature parkland. The rooms smelled of good furniture polish, the Head was imposing, immaculate and perfectly friendly in a formal way, and she asked searching but not prying questions before handing her over to a sixth-form prefect to show her round. The girl was well mannered, well spoken, well briefed.

She was given coffee and biscuits and the opportunity to ask her own questions, the atmosphere of the school was calm, orderly and well presented, and when Olive was shown out, she wanted not to walk but to run down the tree-lined drive to the gates. She felt a desperate, churning panic to get away and not only because the place reminded her of a smarter St Jude's. She found it hard to work out exactly why she had felt so anxious, as if she might be trapped there and never allowed to emerge into the normal, messy, confusing world again. A bus took her slowly, bumpily into the town, where she found a corner to herself in a tea shop with a view of the square, of people moving briskly about, shopping, stopping to talk, queuing for buses, queuing for fresh bread and fish. Her anxiety faded. If Beechway College offered her the post she would not accept, and if they did not she would feel no disappointment.

There had been no mention of literature, books, reading, the English syllabus or even their preferred style of teaching. She had been told about the daily routine, sporting attainments, the background of the pupils, even the uniform, as well as where she herself would live if given the post, about the staff quarters, the washing facilities, the school bicycles which could be borrowed. Nothing about why she had studied and wanted to teach literature, what had formed her and what fired her. The good furniture polish had brought up a shine and a pleasant smell not only on the banisters and the parquet floors but on the rows of pristine books in the library, set spine precisely to spine, not only on the gleaming shoes but on the shiny faces of the girls she met and the eager politeness with which they stood back against the wall to let her pass and opened doors for her. There was an absence of rush, no apparent trouble or discomfort, nothing but an orderly and cheerful existence. It was a school lifted from books she had read at the age of eleven. She had longed for such schools to exist but never quite believed that they did. She had yearned to be sent away to such a boarding school while secretly glad that she was at her own girls' grammar, where everyone left at four, to stream down the hill to the bus station.

She shivered. A woman went past the window, pushing a new pram. Olive turned her head and mind away, in a reflex she had perfected over the past year and a half.

She had always known that she would teach, not because it was her best available option but because she had the passion of an evangelist for winning converts to literature. Books had been all to her. They had saved her and she longed to explain how, and what. The idea of spending her working life dedicated to what she knew and loved best was powerful. She knew instinctively that she would only be any good at teaching those who wanted to learn, who were clever, enthusiastic and willing. Controlling the badly behaved or trying to force an interest in books into uninterested, unreceptive heads would break her. She would only respond to them with impatience and frustration. She imagined that the girls at Beechway College would be well behaved, dull, dutiful, and impervious to a real passion for any book, author, play or poem. They would be attentive but with opaque minds and little imagination.

The Barr School for Girls was in the middle of Salisbury, and had been founded in the late-nineteenth century by one of the admirable fighters for the female right to education. Its core of Victorian buildings had been extended to east and west as far as it could be before it came up against other houses, now mainly converted to offices. Entrance to Beechway College was via an interview and sufficient income. To the Barr it was via a challenging exam. A few scholarships and bursaries were awarded to those of academic excellence but also to those from families with modest means. The girls flew high, music and drama flourished, sport was kept in its place.

The day she walked up the flight of stone steps to the front door, she felt intimidated, challenged, and desperate to be accepted.

*   *   *

'Our daily lives here are not ruled by bells.'

The head, Miss Avril Dauncey, smart, pleasant. Formidable. Olive knew she had to prove herself. At her first college interview she had felt as if she were a performing animal and that the panel of four were only waiting to catch her out, fail her and move on to the next girl. Today she might, probably would, fail but not before she had been given every opportunity to show herself at her best and succeed.

As they stood in the entrance hall, the hands of the Waterloo clock moved to eleven.

Ten seconds later, doors started opening along the corridor ahead and girls streamed out, carrying books and bags, and the noise and the laughter and the sound of footsteps catapulted her back ten years. If their Head had been in sight they, like the Beechway girls, had pressed themselves against walls to let her pass, eyes lowered. These girls smiled, said 'Good morning' and went on their purposeful way, confident, friendly, respectful but not deferential. A minute later, as she was shown into the Head's office, the corridors had fallen silent again. One pair of running footsteps. A banged door. Silence again.

A pot of coffee, milk, sugar, biscuits on a side table. Two cups.

'Please help yourself – no rush, enjoy your biscuit.'

But she did not risk one, embarrassed that she

might choke, spill crumbs, be unable to swallow because she was so nervous.

'Tell me about yourself. I have all your qualifications and so on here of course, but I want to know why you have decided to teach. What is it that makes you want to spend your days imparting knowledge of English literature to adolescent girls? What is it that appeals to you – as a way of life? Because that is what teaching is, you know.'

Half an hour passed. What she felt. How literature had affected her since childhood. Excited her. Formed her. Saved her – though she did not say that. The books, the poems, the writers, the words, the words. She almost tripped over herself, she stuttered in her determination to express it. Miss Dauncey leaned back, fingertips in a steeple, eyes steady on Olive. Listening. Listening and not once interrupting.

She wound down. Faltered and took a deep breath. Felt her face flush. But she had meant it, all of it, it was what she believed – no, knew, and if it was not acceptable, she could not help that or change or retract a word.

She finished her cold coffee.

'It is a joy to hear you talk with such passion. A real joy. I'm a historian and I love my subject, Miss Piper, but a Head is caught up in a lot of administration.

130

I was so afraid of losing touch with history, losing that love, that I decided to make time to teach two classes a week – a first year and a sixth form. It isn't a lot but it keeps me grounded in teaching and thank you for reminding me that a passion for one's subject is nothing to be coy about. Now, have some more coffee? In a couple of minutes, Miss Pengelly, the Head of English, and Miss Neale, her Deputy, will come in. I shall stay but remain silent. Are you happy with that?'

She warmed to Miss Neale, the Deputy, and turned to her with relief after the Head of English had finished questioning her – not that the questions were difficult to answer. They were an attempt to get her to reveal her best side.

'You do not have to love it to teach it well but it gives you a tremendous advantage, and you certainly have to know it.'

'It is far better not to pretend . . . they will always find you out in any case. What you have to do is come clean – say that this or that book or author is not to your personal taste but still explain why it is regarded as great literature. Reading between the lines, I gather you are not particularly enamoured of Keats? Don't worry . . . but his poems are almost always on the O-level syllabus. How do you think you would tackle them?'

Thea Pengelly. She was a woman whose age it was almost impossible to guess. Later, Olive discovered a shy, gentle and very private person beneath the cool exterior, shrewd, sensitive to others and understanding of their needs and weaknesses, and able to win and retain their loyalty and trust – and affection. Somewhere hidden was also a sadness, perhaps a loneliness, to which no one was ever allowed access and with which no one could tamper.

Sylvia Neale was easy, straightforward, or so it seemed this first day, a small woman in a tweed skirt and a blouse with a bow, smiling encouragement. Olive felt herself looking to her instinctively for reassurance and approval and receiving both.

When they left the room, she felt warmed by Miss Neale's friendliness, given out with smiles and nods. Miss Pengelly's reserve made her more difficult to read. She could only wait.

Another prefect. Another tour of a school.

'Have you enjoyed it here?' The girl, who planned to study medicine, smiled and said that she had, 'and I'm proud to have been here as well', and made it sound quite without primness or priggishness, but simply honest.

'Is there anything else you would like to know before you leave?' But there was nothing and she would hear within a week. If she was not offered the post, she knew, as she went back into the street, that she would be disappointed, she wanted it a great deal, for reasons not all of which were immediately clear. She had liked and respected the Head but she would not have a great deal of everyday contact with her. She would be able to relax with Miss Neale, and in Miss Pengelly she recognised a dedicated teacher with high standards, and a rather private woman. But reserved people interested her.

21

A STRETCH OF the town's medieval wall was still intact, inside which courts and alleyways and narrow traffic-free streets were clustered, and there, to her surprise, she found a flat to rent. She had to climb three steep flights of stairs, but once at the top, she had three rooms that might have been in a house in Paris. There were two sloping roof lights, a small sitting room, curtained-off kitchen area, a bedroom overlooking the park, which was lined with horse chestnut trees still heavy with dark green leaves when she moved in but soon to flush golden brown and spatter conkers down onto the paths, a sound she could sometimes hear at night. She could barely afford the rent, on her probationary teacher's salary, and the flat was unfurnished save for an elderly gas cooker and some oak shelving but she had money which her father had sent to her almost two years previously, for James. When she withdrew the first £50 she felt as if she were stealing from her son and half wanted to ask her father's permission to spend any of it. But she did not. She went out and bought a small, old sofa with dusty blue velvet covers, a work table and chair, a bed and some lamps and a few kitchen utensils. It was not a great deal but because the rooms were so small with thick walls and deep sills even this much furniture transformed them into a living space that wrapped itself round her and made her feel safe. She thought of the contrast between this and her father and Peggy's bright flat without character, overlooking the restless sea.

She had got the letter inviting her to take up the teaching post within two days of the interview, after which she had spent part of the summer with Margaret and her husband and small son, in York, a similar medieval-walled city. She got a job selling ice creams outside the Minster during the day and working in a coffee bar on four evenings. She gave Margaret rent, because they struggled on inadequate money, and saved the rest. When she was not working she read and made notes on forthcoming lessons and occasionally remembered her lack of experience and training and panicked. It seemed vaguely wrong that the simple possession of a degree, however good, qualified her to teach clever girls. But she was grateful that it did.

2 2

THE FIRST six weeks drained her of energy and concentration though not for a moment of her enthusiasm. She went straight from school to her flat, and slept for an hour or more, before eating, marking and preparing for the next day. Then she went to bed and woke every morning in need of another two or three hours' sleep. But the pleasure she got from teaching came immediately. The first year, uniform still too big, hair neatly tied back or plaited, were like young animals waiting to be fed by hand, shiny, eager, and so she began by asking them to find a poem – one they already knew or had discovered, which they liked so much that they wanted to learn it by heart, and did so, reciting it to the rest of the class before explaining their choice.

Childhood verses would come to the fore, because

surely they had read little poetry beyond them. 'The Highwayman', 'The Listeners', 'A Smuggler's Song'. All of these came, but also 'The Way Through the Woods', several poems from *A Child's Garden of Verses*, 'Skimbleshanks the Railway Cat', and from one girl, a haunting, bleak little poem by Thomas Hardy – 'At the Railway Station, Upway'. Another had found Yeats's 'Innisfree', because her mother had often talked about 'a bee-loud glade'.

They enjoyed themselves. So did she.

'Have you got a poem, Miss Piper?'

They sat up, expectant, bright-eyed.

'You might find this difficult the first time you hear it but I've made a copy for each of you so you can read it as often as you like, and then write me a page about it for next week please.'

She read them Donne. 'Death be not proud'. They listened. Solemn. Intent. Puzzled. When she handed out the copies, they all began to read it at once. She was lifted up by the way they were engaged by it, however difficult.

She was brought down to earth that afternoon by having to introduce a selection of Gerard Manley Hopkins to her A-level class. She had barely known any Hopkins herself but had been keen to grasp, to learn. To love.

She hated. Overblown. Overwrought. Filled with misery which tipped over into self-pity. She anticipated an hour of trying to analyse, sympathise, explain. Defend. There were only fourteen in this English set and when she walked into the classroom her immediate realisation was that she was not many years older than them. They were like the first years, willing to engage, serious, frowning with concentration, ready to take Hopkins to their hearts.

They hated him too. She knew after a few minutes that she was floundering, failing, doing injustice to the man and his verse by allowing her own prejudice and distaste to show themselves.

The class were uneasy, took dutiful notes, asked no questions and filed out of the room at the end of the lesson looking both baffled and bored.

Olive sat on in the empty classroom, staring down at her book, '*No worst, there is none . . .*', and felt despair. They had chosen her to teach here over several – perhaps many – others and she was out of her depth and dreading the next lesson, although it was Shakespeare's *Measure for Measure*, a play with meat on it, about which they could argue and scrap for the whole period. She felt judged, as if the clever, beady-eyed A-level pupils had seen through her and recognised an impostor.

*   *   *

She was ill at ease walking into the staffroom, where everyone was already in conversation, pouring coffee, lighting cigarettes, at home among familiar colleagues. They were so much older. She remembered hanging about outside the staffroom of her own school waiting to hand something in and feeling that beyond the door, with its frosted-glass panel, lay another and forbidden world, as closed to her as her father's Masonic meetings, which turned a mundane hotel conference room into the Devil's den. 'Olive – I've been wanting a word with you – we need to meet and go over all your classes. How are you finding your feet?'

Thea Pengelly. Taller than Olive. There was the reserve again, but part of it was a stillness about her which made her feel calm and more confident in her turn. The other woman's eyes seemed to search her face for something.

'I don't suppose for a moment we have coinciding free periods this week, do we? Anyway, you look as if you've settled in very happily but if you have any problem at all, come to me. You know the departmental meeting is on Friday?'

'No.'

She gestured. 'That's the noticeboard you need to look at. But the secretary will have put a note in your pigeonhole too.'

Olive had not realised that she had a pigeonhole.

Thea Pengelly was smiling. She touched Olive's arm. 'It takes time to learn the system. I've been here for nine years and I still get caught out, don't worry. Half past four on Friday in the small meeting room.'

'Miss Piper, may I ask you something please? It won't take a minute.'

The rest of the lower fifth were on their way out of the door. Games. Library. Prep room. Tea. Home. Hilary Maidment hovered, book bag at her feet, textbook open. Olive remembered hovering in just such a way herself, usually after an impenetrable Maths lesson, trying to seem nonchalant while almost in tears.

'Yes, of course, but I have a meeting in five minutes.'

'It's . . . this Hopkins poem. I just don't understand it at all.' She held out the open book.

Nor do I, she wanted to say, heaven help me, nor do I.

'I know, Hilary – Hopkins isn't straightforward. I will try and break down line by line any of the set poems people are finding difficult.'

The girl looked doubtful.

'I have to go, I'm afraid.'

'Yes, thank you. Thanks, Miss Piper. I'm sorry.'

'No need to be . . . are there any of the poems you do understand and like?'

'"Felix Randal". I love that. It's as if you get to know him, and maybe "The Windhover". And . . .' She was leafing through her book as they went into the corridor.

'Hilary . . .'

'Yes?'

The girl looked straight at her and there was something in her eyes that Olive found alarming. A look of . . . no. No, she didn't know.

'Thank you so much, Miss Piper. Thank you. I . . . I do love your lessons.'

She stood hopeless in the corridor as Olive sped away, got lost, doubled back. Hilary had gone.

There were six in the English department, and all of them in the room. One, Mrs Dyer, was part-time. She taught remedial English to those she referred to as 'illiterate scientists'. The only one Olive had not met before was Miss Moss, retiring at the end of the term, after having been away for several months because of serious illness, which had culminated in an operation. She smiled, in a tired way, and looked like a revenant, small, frail, with paper-white skin and a detachment from the rest, which she seemed to emphasise by sitting a little apart, her chair pulled away from the desk.

She is dying, Olive thought. She has one foot across the line Death has drawn, and half a mind in another world.

She sat next to Miss Neale, who beamed at her and patted her hand, and said, 'Now we're all grown-ups in here and I am Sylvia and Olive is a very good name. I like Olive. You know the others . . . Pauline – Mrs Dyer – and here's Thea.'

She patted Olive's hand again and sat up, cleared her throat, looking at Miss Pengelly with an eagerness Olive found very appealing.

She felt that she had no right to be here, in a room full of grown-ups. That is what teachers were by definition, surely. When would it come, the ability to feel naturally at home among them, if it had not come by the age of twenty-three, with a degree and a son?

Sylvia Neale was asking to be relieved of teaching the second Shakespeare play on the A-level syllabus and to take on the Hardy novel instead. If she could only be relieved of Hopkins . . .

'Would you care to take on *Macbeth*, my dear?' Miss Neale smiled encouragingly. Olive did not know how to refuse, and in any case, *Macbeth* ought to be fun to teach.

'Olive, if I may, don't take on too much. That's a meaty A-level course you have already – give up something in exchange.'

'Oh. Yes. I see. Yes, of course . . .'

'May I have the Hardy novel?' Miss Neale's face was bland and innocent and Olive's own must have registered her immediate regret.

'Of course. Please do.'

'I'm not at all sure your heart is in that exchange,' Thea Pengelly said. 'And you don't have to make it. I'll take *Macbeth* – heaven knows I've taught it often enough. You keep your Hardy.'

The smile she gave at that moment was one Olive could not interpret, and which stayed with her. She remembered it. She thought about it. She was puzzled by it. Pleased. It had been conspiratorial. No. Amused? Friendly, anyway.

And something else. Something else.

What else?

They were discussing the final choice of school play for the following summer. She listened but did not hear. She heard but did not take in the meaning of the words. She felt as if something had happened but did not know what. Change. That was all. Some change.

'Olive? You have a say too, you know . . . are you happy with that?'

She looked at Thea Pengelly for a long moment. Happy. Happy with that. Happy with . . .

She could not stop looking at her face.

Happy?

'Oh . . . yes, yes of course. I'm perfectly happy with it.'

The play chosen was *The Crucible*.

23

Because the teaching days still tired her, she ignored a feeling of being both physically and mentally drained from the moment she got up one morning in November. She drank three cups of tea but did not want to eat. Her body ached and she began to shiver during the first lesson. By lunch an axe seemed to be splitting her head in two repeatedly and on her way to the staffroom she had to hold on to the wall for fear of falling.

'Home,' the nurse said. She felt too weak to argue. Thea Pengelly drove her back and usually, even at the end of a full day, Olive ran up the three flights of stairs to her flat, but now, she had to pause every other step, while Thea held her arm and murmured encouragement until she reached the top.

Her temperature had been 102 when the nurse took it.

'And coming up these stairs will have made that worse. Do you have any aspirin?'

No.

Yes.

Did she?

'Right, you get into bed. I'm going to the chemist but I'll get you a jug of water first. You need to drink plenty. I'll leave the door on the latch. When you've had the aspirin you need to sleep and I'll call back after school to check on you.'

'But . . . I'm . . . I'll be . . .'

'No,' Thea said, 'you will not be fine.'

Olive remembered little about the following week. At some point a doctor was sitting beside her bed. At some point, her mother was too, or so it seemed. She was in a vortex of nightmares and waking delirium, unable to distinguish between the real and the hallucinatory. The room was dark and then light. The curtains were half open or closed. Sometimes she was alone, at others Thea Pengelley was in the room, sitting beside her or giving her sips of water, helping her to the bathroom, remaking her bed. She could not understand why the Head of Department was looking after her but she felt too ill to ask questions.

She slept for most of the days and tried, but failed, to eat soup or bread and butter which Thea brought to her. Mornings merged into evenings, darkness became light, her life seemed to be on a perpetual loop and her head ached so that she could not think for long about anything. Her chest hurt. She had a relentless cough which pulled at her muscles and left her gasping and exhausted after each bout.

And then, she woke one morning to the sun touching the opposite wall and a sense that she was beginning to emerge from a tunnel, still confused, still too weak to get out of bed without help, but with a feeling of being in clear water. Her headache had gone, leaving only a fogginess in her brain, and her cough was easier.

She turned her head. She saw a pale sky. Her dressing gown on the chair. A jug of water with slices of lemon floating. A card propped up on the tumbler.

'*I will be back at 1.15. T.*'

She struggled to grasp who, what, when.

T.

She felt limp but, at the same time, rinsed clean. She was sure she had no temperature.

She would go to the bathroom and brush her teeth, wash herself with a flannel. Perhaps she would feel strong enough to have a bath tomorrow. But when she put her feet on the floor and then stood upright, the room lurched, the light spun round and she could not get her breath. She flopped back onto her bed but the effort of pulling the covers over herself was quite beyond her. She slept, face down on the pillow. Sleep blotted everything out.

That evening, if it was the evening, she woke to find that she was propped up on her pillows, the lamp switched on beside her bed, and Thea sitting in the chair, marking a pile of books.

'Oh . . .'

Thea smiled, putting down her pen.

'What time is it?'

'Just after seven o'clock. You look better.'

'I think . . . I feel better. How long have I been like this?'

'Ill? Nine days.'

It made no sense. Perhaps two – three at the most. Not nine days.

'When did you come?'

'I've been here on and off all the time. I went into school most days and then Sylvia Neale came in my place. I don't think you were ever aware of her, were you? She thought not.'

Olive tried to think but her brain would not process the information.

'Would you like a drink or something to eat?'

Would she?

Without warning, Olive burst into tears, tears that bubbled up out of weakness and illness, and something like shame.

'I'm sorry,' she said, 'I'm so sorry.'

Thea dropped her books, and came and put her arms round her, and held her.

24

So it had not only been Thea who had looked after her. Olive barely remembered. She was simply aware of a lift of the heart when she saw Thea. She was puzzled by it, but only knew that in Thea's presence she felt safe.

One evening, when she was recovering steadily, she sat in the window with *The Mayor of Casterbridge* open beside her. Her brain still felt fragile, as if it would crack open like an egg if she concentrated too hard for too long, so she read slowly and paused every few pages, realising that her mind and memory were still intact and only needed strengthening, like the muscles of her body.

'You've got some colour in your cheeks – how good to see that!' Thea held a small box of oranges.

'Why have you been doing all this for me?'

Thea glanced away, took the fruit into the kitchen and did not come out again for several minutes. Olive heard the sound of the kettle being filled, the chink of the china teapot. She heard cutting sounds. Then the smell of freshly squeezed oranges came through the door.

Why?

Thea brought in a glass of juice, and handed it to her, fussed about with the tea things. She seemed ill at ease.

'Why?'

Her face was turned away but the light caught one side of her hair, her forehead and cheekbone and mouth, and Olive realised that, just as when she had been at school considering her own teachers, she had assumed Thea to be much older than she could now see that she was. Teachers had all been over fifty, some of them over sixty, other than the young games staff, older beyond imagining. Thea was probably in her early forties, no more. She had dark hair, rather unruly, kept back with a comb on either side. Her bones were fine, nose small, cheekbones high.

She looked away.

Silence. A long silence. A stillness in the room. A charged stillness. She did not understand it.

Something would happen. Something might be

said, and if so, it might take a long time but that would not matter. It would be said.

'You feel it too,' Thea said at last. 'Or am I wrong about this? Because if I am please say so now . . . in the next thirty seconds . . .'

Olive said nothing. But without warning, her mind sprang forwards, to Christmas.

'Christmas,' she said.

She supposed that she would be expected to go to her father but even the thought of moving anywhere made her head hurt and spending a ritual few days in the bright box apartment would test all her reserves.

But she should go.

'What will you do?'

She supposed that Thea had parents and siblings, an extended family of some kind, but she had no idea at all. She did not even know where she lived. And who with, if anyone.

There was silence again. But not tense this time, or awkward, silence like a pillow that could be rested upon. Stillness.

Then, into the silence and the stillness she had an urge to place something – almost like a gift. It was not a confession nor the telling of any secret, it was like an object, a fact which had substance and great power.

Thea seemed scarcely to be breathing.

She reached out her hand and put it on top of Olive's own hand and they sat in silence, until Olive said, 'Two years ago, my son was born. His name was James but perhaps it isn't now. They may have given him another name. The people who adopted him. Yes, they probably have.'

After the terrible day at St Jude's when she had found him gone from the nursery, she wondered if she had ever really cried for him out of a full heart or had merely pushed down most of her tears and covered them with a lid of steel, for fear of losing control altogether. She had cried, she had been sad, and shocked by his abrupt disappearance, she had regretted everything but she had never submerged herself almost to drowning, stripping her mind of every other thought, herself of every other feeling.

She did so now and Thea knelt beside her and held her and said nothing at all.

When she eventually surfaced, she felt scoured and raw, and the room was dark, and she knew that whatever this was now, it was all she had, and it was right. She did not grasp her own feelings fully or recognise Thea's, she was simply content to accept them, whatever their nature, and be still.

'Spend Christmas here. With me,' Olive said.

There was a silence and then Thea got up. 'Or

shall we just leave all of that for now? You're exhausted enough without having to think about Christmas. I'll make a few very small and delicious sandwiches to tempt you, and then you should go back to bed.'

'I'm so sorry – I'm really not hungry.'

'You will be when you see the smallness of these . . . one bite each. Go on. I'll bring your tray.'

She ate three of the minute sandwiches and then Thea left, and after she had gone, Olive lay awake, asking questions.

What was this? She was not so ignorant or naive as to be completely unaware – remembering the women her mother had referred to obliquely, those with shingled hair and men's evening suits. But they were in the past. This was different. Different.

So, what was this? While she had been half asleep, half absent, in illness, what had happened?

She slept then, and dreamed of the nursery at St Jude's. She walked into it and round it and there were many cots, dozens of cots, and every cot was empty.

The next morning she got up, washed and dressed, and then collapsed into her chair and read *The Mayor of Casterbridge* and for the first time managed to concentrate on it for over an hour.

She came out of the novel in a panic. She was alone

but soon might not be and she felt troubled and bewildered. Whatever it was, she decided she wanted none of it, and wrote her father a note saying that she would love to join them for Christmas, that she had been ill and would value some quiet time spent in their apartment.

The idea of going downstairs and along the street to the letter box was daunting but she put on her coat and scarf. She wanted to smell the outside air. She opened the door and stepped out and her head swam, her legs gave way under her. Thea, just arriving, caught her the second before she fell.

25

THE JOURNEY tired her so much that when she reached the flat she went straight to bed and slept until mid-morning on Christmas Eve.

'You've lost so much weight, Livi, and you were never fat. You need sea air and good food.'

He touched her arm. He was pleased that she had come, she could tell, and Peggy had welcomed her more warmly than before. She had had no chance to shop for presents and felt conscious of arriving empty-handed but they both brushed her apologies aside. There was a small artificial tree in the corner, with one or two of the old decorations on it that she remembered from childhood, as well as new ones, and she was touched that when so much had been cleared from the old house, these had been kept.

'I have booked us Christmas Day lunch at the de

Vere, Livi. I don't want Peggy working away in the kitchen all morning and there isn't much room in there for me to help her. I'm afraid I have become rather lazy where cooking is concerned and we eat out quite a bit.'

Her mother had cooked a large Christmas dinner to which they had sat down at two o'clock, and the effort of preparing for it and providing it and insisting that every detail was correct had always put her into a bad mood, slamming pots down, breaking china, refusing to speak at the table. It had been a miserable occasion and Olive had dreaded it and dreamed of the future when she had her own house and kitchen. And family, she supposed.

And after all, the hotel proved a good idea. It was festive, fun, cheerful and good to watch others. 'People spying' Peggy called it. In the flat, they would have made false conversation. Here, it seemed easy, in the noise of the dining room, with families and children as well as couples. The food, what she could eat of it, was good but her appetite was still poor.

And all the time, all the time, she was in a frenzy of uncertainty and emotion. She tried to push the thoughts away, to switch them off as they ran like moving messages through her head, tried to replace the images with others from other times of her life. But she could not. In the end, the feelings drove her to say, early on Boxing Day morning, that she wanted to walk by the sea a little, on her own.

'There is so much to think about and plan for the start of term. Besides, it will give you some time together.'

So far as she knew they spent most of every day and every night with just one another. If they had made new friends, none were ever mentioned.

It was cold and clear, the sea like bottle glass and she did as she had been bidden and took deep lungfuls of air. People walked smartly, believing that it was doing them good. She could not and several times she leaned on the railings to look at the sea, but not seeing it, seeing always, Thea.

She had never been in love, nor, so far as she knew, had anyone loved her – certainly not Malcolm, though he had liked her, perhaps been fond of her. If they had married, perhaps they might have been happy enough. Who knew? Perhaps it had been his parents who had wanted it, pushed him to ask her. Perhaps he had tried to defy them. If so, she would have respected him for it.

No. She walked on. Not 'enough'. People should not marry to be 'happy enough'. Because she had never fallen in love she had never been sure what to expect, only that she would recognise that it had happened when the time came. So, was it this? This overwhelming desire to see someone, be with them, and to tell them everything, all the truth that had ever been told. Was it talking to them in your head, as she did now, as if they were never not there? She traced Thea's features, eyes, nose, mouth, her hair, her hands, in her mind.

Yet she had run away. Whatever this was, it filled her with fear and embarrassment and the strange sense of being doomed. It was not usual. It was frowned upon. It disturbed her profoundly. She thought that she ought not to go back, but give in her notice, on the grounds of ill health, and loss of nerve for teaching. She could return to the flat to pack up. It would take her only a couple of days and she would not step outside the door or see anyone at all.

Why should she do this? What was she afraid of?

She sat on a bench and turned her coat collar up against the wind.

Of what people might say. Would say. What they would think. How they would judge her.

But how much would those things matter?

Of taking the wrong road, then, and missing the right one.

Of following her feelings, which might turn out to be like a house built upon the sand.

Of ruining her career, her promising career, when

it had barely begun. It was the right career, that was the one thing of which she was certain.

Of Thea.

Yes.

No.

Not of Thea herself, but of the power of Thea's own feelings, which might sway her against her rational judgement, and take her in the wrong direction.

What was that? What was the right direction?

She got up and walked on as quickly as she could, because she was cold and because her head was bursting.

There was no one at all she could talk to, except perhaps Margaret, who had never given pat replies or put the conventional view. She thought things through. She gave her own opinion.

She could not travel up to York. But she could write.

That evening, she made half a dozen attempts at starting a letter but always stopped when she reached the point of telling. Confessing? Asking. Every phrase she wrote sounded either clinical or evasive and when she read them on the page, read her own handwriting, she felt exposed and awkward.

Ashamed?

But in the end, she chose what seemed the least

embarrassing, more matter-of-fact phrases, and sent the letter.

She went back to the flat after another couple of days. The time with her father and Peggy had been easier than she had expected, she had felt more at home, less tense, though she had still tired easily.

Had they enjoyed having her to stay? They were polite, they told her to go back as often as she liked, but she sensed that they were happy in the small world of their apartment, happy and close. Perhaps more than her father and Evelyn had ever been.

It was unnerving to be back home. She had only a swirling fog of memories of being ill there and she felt like a stranger in the rooms, which seemed dark after the seafront flat. Little seemed familiar and what did reminded her of a long-past life. The sense of dislocation would lessen, she knew, and that she would be perfectly well enough to return to school the following week.

Except for Thea.

Thea had not ceased to occupy every corner of her mind and every waking minute and to fill her dreams.

Thea.

*   *   *

She went over and over the wording of her resignation letter. It must be simple and clear – and definite. There was the question of a reference. She intended to go to a school in some distant part of the country, she had no idea yet where, but there would be advertisements to which she would respond. Could she ask for a reference after such a short time at Barr's? Her illness was not her fault and would surely not be held against her, but there must be other good and credible reasons why she should leave. Perhaps she did not really care. She thought only of Thea and Thea was not a reason to which she could ever admit.

She switched on the lamps. There was a small pile of books beside the chair. Peggy had sent her back with a package of food, eggs, cold meat, some leftover cheeses and a slab of the Christmas cake.

She would eat, and then write the letter.

Eat the eggs. Eat some cake. Write the letter.

Make a cup of tea and write the letter.

Settle down and then write the . . .

The doorbell rang once, as if someone had pressed it gently.

There was a flicker of a moment in which Olive knew that she had to choose and that once the choice was made she would never have it or any power over its consequences again. The flicker of a moment was out of time, as such moments generally are. It lasted an hour or a day or a lifetime or the fragment of a second. She had endless time in which to decide, all the time that was or had been or would be for the rest of her life. She had a flicker of time in which to be born and grow and live and die, in which to choose whether to leave and never once look back or acknowledge that this had been.

She had a flicker of time in which to refuse.

To accept.

Yes.

Afterwards, it seemed to her that she had never had a choice but had been quite powerless all along, but that was not true, she simply forgot.

She lit the fire and they sat together beside it and when Thea touched her, reaching over and taking her hand, Olive understood at once that she had never been touched before or never felt herself respond before.

'How did you know I was back?'

'I didn't . . .' Thea stroked her hair. 'I came past every day, to see if there was a light.'

They talked then, of each other, of their pasts, hopes, dreads. Of love, but not yet of lovers.

'What will we do?' Olive sat up, the reality of it making her heart race. 'What will happen?'

Thea was silent for a moment and when Olive

looked at her she saw both thoughtfulness and also anxiety, on the face she now loved.

'Nothing will happen. We found one another.'

'Yes, but there can't be any future for us.'

'Of course there can! What are you afraid of – what people might think? Or say? But people needn't know.'

'No, but they will find out.'

'No, because we won't tell them or make it obvious.'

'All the same . . . won't it be best if I just leave the school? I was going to resign anyway.'

'Why?' Thea drew back from her.

'Because of this . . . You. I didn't even know if you . . . I didn't know anything, Thea. I couldn't bear to be with you every day if I had just made some stupid mistake . . . fantasy . . . I don't know. It just seemed best to resign.'

'I love you. There. Will you leave now?'

'Leave you?'

'The school.'

'Yes. It's even more important now, isn't it?'

'I don't know . . . and that is the truth. But – perhaps.'

'There are plenty of schools.'

'None as good, not for a long way, and you don't want to take any old teaching job, you're too good.'

'I'll get another sort of job.'

'No, you won't. You won't do anything. Not yet. Not in a rush.'

'Where will you be?'

'Be?'

'Live. I want to live with you.'

'I don't think so, darling. That would be too obvious. We have to be aware of other people, even if we disagree with them – of what they think, what they say.'

'So I will stay in the flat?'

'Yes. Please don't worry. And don't be afraid of anyone or anything.'

'No.'

No.

When Thea left at one o'clock that morning, slipping quietly down the stairs and out into the silent lane, Olive lay in her bed, awake and awake, feeling herself to be wholly new-born and barely known.

She returned to school and the first department meeting of the term and sat on the far side of the table, to Thea's left, so that it would be impossible to catch her eye.

'My dear Olive, how very good to have you back! Are you quite better? You're very *thin*.'

Sylvia patted her shoulder, her face creased with smiles and goodwill, sat next to her and went on smiling, as she smiled encouragingly to girls who blushed and stammered when asked to read aloud. A good woman, Olive thought, looking at Sylvia's jade-green beads which had one in the string missing, and the buttons on her blouse whose top two buttons were done up the wrong way. She remembered that they had laughed at Miss Barlow, who always had something wrong with her clothing, and pins falling out of her hair. And she had been a good, kind woman too and they had never seen it, too busy as they always were to snigger at her getting awkwardly onto her bicycle and sailing off down the road, with her hair gradually coming undone.

What would Sylvia say, if she knew? Would she be shocked into silent disapproval, or be generous and understanding?

Thea was talking about the A-level syllabus – too many Victorians, too much that was tired and obvious. 'The Old Faithfuls.' Olive agreed but said nothing and did not even glance up.

'And one more thing – we need to wake up lower four B. They're like rows of suet puddings. Has anyone else managed to get a spark out of them? No, I thought not. Isn't it odd how it goes like this . . . one class is sparkling with eagerness and enthusiasm and another is like the walking dead. If anyone can suggest a book that will set them alight?'

'*Dr Jekyll and Mr Hyde*,' Olive said, without having meant to say anything at all.

Thea looked round at her and away again. 'That's an idea – it isn't long but there's plenty of meat on it . . . lots to discuss.'

'Well suggested!' Sylvia said. The little pat on her arm again. Olive felt her face heat.

They moved on to talk about the production of *The Crucible*.

26

THEA CAME to the flat every other day and on Sundays they drove out to walk over the Downs, sometimes in bitter winds, but where they saw no one they knew and they felt free and untroubled. They found pubs in which to drink whisky and warm themselves, before returning to Thea's car, and Olive felt that the strangers they came upon must see at once that she was lit up by love, that it was visible, forming around her like phosphorescence, and when she looked into Thea's eyes she saw that they reflected the same joy.

'Why am I not allowed to see where you live?' she asked suddenly, as they sat watching the rain sluice down the car windows. Veils of it hid the hills.

'Of course you're allowed! Listen, I am only trying to spare you. I have never said anything because – well, actually, I suppose there is no good reason. But my mother lives with me and she is confused now, and anyone she doesn't know worries her. She can't cope with any sort of novelty, or disturbance . . . she's fine when she's among familiar things and with people she knows. That's all.'

'But . . . I'm sorry. I wasn't prying.'

'There's no such thing – not between us. How could there be? Of course I should have told you . . . it was stupid and you must have thought it very odd.'

'In a way. It doesn't matter now I know.'

'I wasn't trying to shut you out.'

'No, and I understand. Of course I do . . . Is she alone all the time when you're at school?'

'Not all the time . . . we have good neighbours and someone goes in every day to get her lunch and generally keep her company. She's in her late seventies but her mind is – no age. A child's age again. It's easing off – come on, make a run for it.'

There was only an electric fire in this particular pub but there were good ham sandwiches, and a table in the dimly lit corner.

'I am happy,' Olive said, closing her eyes with the impact of it, 'I am so happy.'

Thea took her hand. 'I wasn't trying to keep secrets.'

'Of course not . . . and some things are not necessarily for telling.'

'I want to tell you everything I can.'

Everything. Olive looked into the glowing red coils of the fire. Everything.

What had she told? Childhood. Her mother. Father. Her mother's death. Peggy. College. Malcolm. *Dr Faustus*. Penny. James.

She felt her hand curled in Thea's. She felt her own happiness.

She felt safe. A new life.

Safe.

She still did not fully understand it all but she no longer felt like running away, or that she should deny it.

She and Thea. Whatever it was, they were. But she had told her the bare facts about James. She had told her about meeting Malcolm. Going out with Malcolm. Staying with his family. And she made light of it all.

Beyond the bare facts, there was a door and it was locked and bolted. James was on the other side. Safe. No one else went there.

James, pink mouth, puckered like a sea anemone round her breast. She all but felt the force of it as the mouth sucked and pulled and there was an answering pull inside her, as well as in her breasts, a tug which was very strong but quite painless.

'What is it?'

She surfaced. Breathed. 'Nothing.'

Thea lifted Olive's hand to her mouth and bit the little finger very gently and there was the same responding tug inside her. Strong. Painless.

They left and ran again through the rain.

And the weeks and months went by in the same haze of joy and disbelief, without any pause for concern or even to think, though the time was punctuated by days when work took first place, and then they simply set their own lives aside safely and gave their whole attention to pupils, lessons, preparation, books, marking, meetings and *The Crucible.*

Thea was directing it and there were two and then three after-school rehearsals a week until Easter. When they came back at the end of April, there would be more.

'The school play,' Thea said, 'takes over.'

'What can I do? I could be on the prompt book. I'm quite good at it.'

'Ah – *Dr Faustus*! I'm sure you are but Sylvia has been on the book for every school play since time began. She would not give it up unless it was prised from her hands – and even then.'

Meanwhile, she had a week when her mother went to stay in a home, she said, always the same one, which she knew and liked.

'A week. Where shall we go?'

Suffolk was milky skies and seal-coloured, gull-coloured shingle and the first curlews mournful across the marshes. They rented rooms overlooking the sea and watched the fishing boats riding in on the waves and lay together hearing the crash and boom of them as the tide came up the beach. Walked. Sat on the sea wall. Talked. Talked.

'Have you always known?'

Thea usually turned her head to look at her when she replied but now she continued to look at the silver line of the horizon.

'No. Well – perhaps. But hidden so deep I could never have dived down to it. And I was married.'

Olive had no idea what to say.

'For six years. He – Philip – taught Classics. We started as trainees in the same school.'

'Did . . . no, it doesn't matter.'

'Ask anything – I don't mind.'

'No. It's not for me to know.'

'I want to tell you everything. And know everything. That's how it is.'

'Yes.'

'There isn't much anyway. We were perfectly happy – we got on well, we shared interests, we liked one another's company – that counts for a lot, you know. I suppose we loved one another. Yes, of course we did. But we were never in love in the way that we should have been. We didn't know that, of course.'

'What happened?'

'I met someone else. And as chance would have it, so did he – at the same time. We parted quite amicably. He died of leukaemia, a couple of years ago.'

Something in her voice indicated that despite her saying she wanted to tell Olive everything, that door had closed. No more would be told her, and she was warned not to ask.

Thea took her hand. 'You might as easily have married Malcolm.'

'I would never have done that.'

'Because you didn't love him?'

'I didn't.'

'It might just have come about – which was more or less what happened to me, with Philip. Us.'

Olive thought of the Crowleys' house. The evening drinks. The tidiness. Their kindness. Penny.

What was happening to them now? Was Thea right, that she might have fallen into marriage? If so, she would have had James now.

But otherwise, marriage would have shrivelled some essential part of her. She sensed that now. And she had Malcolm's foresight, Malcolm's refusal to take the expected, the conventional way out, to thank.

'I'm happy,' she said and leaned in to smell the smell of Thea's coat, her hair, her skin. Her smell. 'If I had been married to Malcolm, this couldn't have happened.'

'No, but something else would. Someone else. You would have discovered.'

'I'm sure I wouldn't.'

'I did.'

She did not say, 'But that is different. You are different.' Because she could not have explained what she meant. But she believed it to be true.

'Where did she go?'

'She?'

'The person you met when you . . . that person.'

Thea jumped down from the wall and held her arms out and Olive jumped, and they stood close together on the shingle and the wind whipped suddenly off the sea and blew their hair. It was cold and clouds were massing, clouds the colour of the gulls and the darkest pebbles.

'Come on.'

They ran, and were out of breath as they reached the front door as the rain began.

Thea went to make tea and Olive stood at the bay window, watching as the storm broke and the waves roared and reared up like great beasts.

And Thea had not answered.

27

THE SCHOOL year ran on. At Easter, which was late, they went to the Scilly Isles for five days and each island was quieter than the last and they walked and sat on deserted beaches, and talked and slept. Thea had to go back to her mother, and at the last minute, Olive decided to stay on, she felt so well, so contented, but on her own, she became melancholy and restless, and took the boat back early, telling Thea in a brief note, '*I miss you. I am only half a person without you.*'

School. Exams. Play rehearsals. Tennis matches. Rounders matches. Wins and losses. Trophies and consolations. The girls sat against the wall of the music block, skirts as high as they dared lift them, browning their legs, heads back and eyes closed against the sun.

She and Thea prised out nuggets of time to spend together – two or three Sundays in the country, occasional evenings in the flat with the windows wide open and, after dark, walking in the town park under the trees, heavy with leaf, where surely no one ever saw them.

'What are we going to do in the summer?'

Thea had an arm round Olive's shoulders and now she pulled her to sit on the bench by the pond, where the odd mysterious sound came from deep in the hidden water. It was warm enough to have come out without jackets.

Olive assumed that although Thea would have to spend some of the time with her mother – probably even take her away somewhere for a week – they would spend long lazy weeks together somewhere.

'Right away would be lovely, wouldn't it? Italy, or Spain?' She could not see Thea's face clearly, but still she sensed doubt. 'But anywhere in this country. I don't mind, even if it rains every day. We would be together.'

'I could perhaps take a week . . . perhaps at the end of July. I have to see to my mother and there are old friends in Scotland I usually go to in August. I'm sorry – were you expecting more? I'm sorry . . .' and she touched Olive's cheek.

'No . . . of course. Anything. I'll visit my father and

Peggy anyway – they'll expect it. When we do go, we won't want anywhere crowded, will we?'

Thea was silent.

'I wondered . . .'

'You wonder an awful lot.'

It felt like a rebuke but the tone of voice was wrong.

'Is there anything we can do next term – about being together? Living together? It's so – it feels so uncertain. Temporary.'

'I know.'

'Is there – which village do you live in?'

It was ridiculous that she still did not know. But Thea laughed.

'Strong Melton . . . everyone asks about the Strong and nobody has any idea.'

'Might there be a cottage or something for me to rent there? Then we could be close to one another without actually living together.'

'We do have to be careful, you know. People talk. And we are teachers.'

'Yes.'

A nightbird made a strange cry from the bushes.

'We have to go,' Thea said.

In the middle of the tension of O and A levels, the normal timetable still continued.

'For those girls between exams, we will put on special classes – music and art appreciation are covered, as usual. The Domestic Science classes for cookery are oversubscribed. I know that, as ever, the English department has its hands full with the play but not everyone is involved.'

There was a full turnout of staff. The main meeting room was packed, and stuffy, though every window had been opened. The Head looked across the table.

'Olive? Do you have anything to offer?'

'I can run a special class in medieval poetry – looking at the language too. And the golden age of detective fiction perhaps? And –'

'Don't take on too much. But those sound ideal. Put up notices asking them to sign up.'

'I'll put up a reading list.'

'They won't have a lot of time – a few of the best detective stories, maybe? Now, PE people . . . cricket. They always love it, and no, we cannot make cricket an official school sport, sorry.'

The meeting was winding down. Thunder rumbled in the distance.

'Miss Piper, do you have a minute?' Hilary, emerging from the shadows of the chapel corridor. She often seemed to be about.

'I was just wondering if I can sign up for your extra classes . . .'

'Not really, no . . . You're lower sixth – these are for the A-level people. You'll get your chance next year.'

'But you might not be doing them next year.'

The girl had wide-open eyes that barely blinked, just gazed at Olive.

'There will be something, I'm sure. Sorry, Hilary.'

If she did not end the conversation and move away immediately, even as she was in the middle of speaking, the girl would have walked alongside her, and more questions would follow, she was a past master at keeping pace as she talked.

'She's like the Ancient Mariner.'

'Hilary is a clever girl,' Thea said. They were finishing supper. 'Just a bit intense. Don't you like her?'

'It's not a question of liking or not liking.'

'Did you never have a crush on a teacher?'

'No.'

'On another girl then?'

'No.'

No. She had thought about it a great deal recently. The answer was always no.

'Hm. Anyway, Hilary is harmless enough – just dodge her, or else come right out with it and tell her to stop ambushing you.'

Thea seemed amused. But it was not amusing. It was annoying. And creepy. And it disturbed her.

'I can't be late back this evening, love.'

'Oh – is your mother all right?'

'A bit querulous – she doesn't like me being out. I'm out all day, remember.'

'Yes.'

'I know it isn't easy. It will get better, I promise. We'll go away.'

'When?'

'I'll look into it . . . the very end of July. Or early August. Hardy country, maybe?'

'Yes!'

'There – that will make you happy.'

'But will it make you happy as well?'

'Of course. Funny girl. Of course it will.'

She went. Olive listened to her footsteps going down the stairs, and then to the car starting. And then to the silence.

She turned back into the room and the miasma came over her, the damp, opaque feeling of having to spend the rest of the evening on her own after all . . . the absence of Thea.

She dug out her textbooks and sat at the table ready to work, but stared into space, without enthusiasm or energy.

She pulled the notepad towards her.

'Darling . . . I hate it when you go. I want you to stay always, and always be with me. We are apart too much. We should never be apart. Please let us find a way? You said you would see if there might be somewhere for me to rent, in your village. Please look. It would be perfect. Better than . . .'

She put the note in Thea's pigeonhole the next morning. Thea had said that she would not be able to come to the flat for a few nights but just after nine that evening her footsteps came on the stairs. She had brought half a lemon meringue pie, a punnet of strawberries, some cream, and they picnicked. Olive was suffused with joy at the surprise of it.

'Your note,' Thea said. 'I'm looking, my dear one, I've asked one or two people, but it isn't easy. It may happen but not overnight.'

'So long as it will. I don't mind how long I wait to be nearer to you. I can wait . . .'

It was after midnight when Thea left.

'Don't come down.'

'Of course I'm coming down. I want every last second of you. You shouldn't have to go.'

Thea looked at her, a long, unblinking look.

'No.'

'There has to be a way. There has to be somewhere. Then you will still be with your mother, but close to me.'

182

'I am always close to you. But you're right . . . and there will be somewhere, surely. Now, go inside. No more illness.'

But it was not Olive who became ill. The message reached her at school the following morning. Thea drove her to the station.

'I wish I could take you all the way there, love, but apart from having to find cover for your classes and all the other things, it would look odd.'

'Would it?'

'Yes. It shouldn't, and it's wrong that we should even have to think like that. One day . . . Let me know how things are.'

'Of course. I'll try and phone you tonight.'

'No, you'll be needed. But drop me a note in a day or two – unless you're back soon and it isn't as bad as it seems.'

But it was bad.

She had not let herself imagine, and Peggy had only left a bare message telling her that she should go down. She was not prepared.

The stroke had paralysed the whole of her father's left side. His arm lay inert as a piece of butcher's meat, on the bedcover. His face was screwed up, the sight blanked out of one eye, his mouth twisted. From time to time he let out an odd little yelp.

'He is in quite a lot of pain,' the Sister said. 'We're giving him what we can. We have to be careful. But we don't want Daddy to suffer.'

Olive winced.

It had happened in the early hours, Peggy said, and at first it seemed nothing, and he had begun to recover. He said it was 'just a funny moment'. But then another. He had fallen.

'Was he conscious?'

Peggy looked away.

Was he conscious now? The right eye had light, but still looked at her vacantly.

The nurse wiped the corner of his mouth and pushed his slack lower lip back into place.

'You sit down,' Peggy said. 'I need to get some air. Will you be all right?'

'Of course.'

She reached for her father's hand. They were in a side room off the main ward. Sounds came. Coughs. The screech of trolley wheels, and rubber-soled shoes on polished floors. Retching. Absolute silence. A voice. A door sucking shut.

His hand felt damp. She turned it over and touched the back. Fine hairs. His signet ring. Familiar hand. She talked to him quietly, telling him about the school, small, remembered incidents, her flat, the books she was reading. He lay, warm and breathing but so heavily still.

'Does he understand me?'

A nurse had come in and was wiping his mouth, feeling his pulse. 'It's hard to know. But he can hear you. They can always hear.'

They.

'I feel as if I'm talking to myself.'

But she shrugged and left.

'I love you very much,' she said, and lifted her father's hand to her cheek. The eye was still bright but did not focus on her. On anything.

Peggy did not come back for over an hour, during which visitors had to leave. Olive waited at the entrance.

'They don't say what's going to happen,' Peggy said, hunched into the taxi seat.

'Probably because they don't know,' Olive replied.

Olive had never seen herself as a strong person, because she had always lacked confidence, never been sure what she should do, which road to take. But in the face of Peggy's shocked subsidence into a sort of inertia and a dependency on her to make all the decisions, she was discovering hidden reserves.

She made an omelette, made tomatoes into a salad, buttered bread. There was only an inch of milk left.

'You eat,' Peggy said, 'I couldn't. What are we

going to do?' She was watching as Olive laid the table. Beyond the glass wall the sea was sullen, lead-grey.

'We can't possibly make any decisions, Peggy . . . it will be a case of taking each day. Come and sit down. Do you have anything to drink – a brandy, or sherry? That would help you.'

'There's a bottle of port and some brandy.'

Olive mixed them, weak for herself but making Peggy's two-thirds brandy. She drank it all.

'You can stay, can't you, Livi?'

'I'm not sure for how long. There's a lot to do as the school term winds down. If you'd rather not be here alone, is there anyone you could stay with?'

'It isn't so much that – but if they send him home.'

'I doubt if they will. He'll need nursing.'

'Yes, and I am not a nurse.'

'Nor am I – nor are most people, come to that. I may have to go back and then come down here again later.'

'I couldn't have him here on my own.' She looked desperately at Olive. She had put on weight. They ate well, often out, and sat about in the apartment a good deal, only strolled along the seafront occasionally. But her hair was set, make-up complete, clothes smart.

'I often wonder about my parents,' Olive said. 'Perhaps everyone does. Parents are so deeply unknown, aren't they? To their children, I mean. Did they love each other, were they happy? My mother was a very closed person.'

Peggy looked startled and as if this was a conversation she could not cope with. But she managed to say, 'He has always spoken about Evelyn with great affection, you know. I have never thought they were anything other than a happy couple.'

'And you? I'm sorry, I put that badly. I meant – do you feel that you made the right choice? Is this the life you wanted?'

For a moment she thought that Peggy might reveal whatever was the truth, about herself, the marriage. It was not that Olive expected any dreadful revelations because it had seemed to her from the beginning that they were well matched, led a life they enjoyed – had contentment. And where was the harm in any of that?

But Peggy got up. 'I'm sorry – I feel absolutely wrung out. I just can't cope with anything.'

'Of course. You go to bed. You need to sleep. I shall stay up and read for a bit. I'll leave my door ajar in case the phone rings. Can I get you anything, Peggy?'

No.

It only took ten minutes to clear away and wash up, and then she stood looking at the sea, mumbling like an old man without teeth, before going to bed, but instead of reading, she decided to write to Thea, needing to tell her about her father's illness, what he looked like, the way it had changed everything, thrown her about like a ship's passenger in a storm. She wanted to make something clear. Don't waste time. Don't wait. Don't harbour secrets. Because what was the point of waiting, wasting, keeping secrets?

She heard Peggy.

'I was hoping you were still up, Livi. I've just been lying there. I can't sleep. Everything is going round in my head. But you're wanting to get to bed . . .'

'No, I'm fine. Shall I make some tea?'

They went into the sitting room. Peggy looked twenty years older, heavy under her eyes and dough-pale without her make-up. Her hair was flat.

The lights winked on and off, from warning buoys out at sea, and a ship crawled along in the distance, like an illuminated snail. They sat watching.

'What were you going to do with your summer holiday?' Peggy said.

What were you going to do? So would she not be going away now? Did Peggy expect her to come here and stay for the whole time?

'I'm going to Dorset – and maybe to France for a week later on.'

'Alone?'

'No.'

'I'm glad. There should be someone in your life, you know. You're young and attractive and good company. Don't become one of those spinster schoolmistresses.'

Olive drank her tea and looked at the dark water.

'Tell me about him . . . I need some nice news to take my mind off everything.'

There was no decision behind it, she had not planned to tell anyone, perhaps Peggy least of all. She did not stop to imagine what her reaction might be, she simply told – not everything, but enough. Told about her own feelings and Thea's and about the present and what they planned to be their future, and as she told, it seemed that Thea was there in the room with them, encouraging, pleased, confirming everything.

She stopped speaking. The room was very silent. Very still. She felt a closeness to her stepmother, a warmth. She had never sensed any real affection between them but now she did. It could not have been by chance that Peggy was the first person to know, except Margaret, in a letter. Margaret had not yet replied.

The ship had slipped out of sight and only the warning buoys blinked on and off, out at sea.

Olive turned her head. Peggy's face was set in an

expression of – of what? She could not decipher, except that it was stiff, unmoving. Marble or stone. She seemed hardly to be breathing.

She knew then.

'Pray God your father never knows. Pray God. And I forbid you to tell him. Let him retain some illusions about you in whatever time he has left.'

She got up and went to the door, head high, and without looking at Olive again, said, 'As if you had not done harm enough by having an illegitimate child. But at least that was natural. At least that was normal. May you be forgiven. I would like you to leave here first thing in the morning and not, please, to see your father again. God knows what you might blurt out.'

For a few moments, after she had gone out of the room, Olive sat quite still, feeling nothing, but then, as if she had been put under a stream of hot water and thawed in an instant, she jumped up, fury burning through her, and banged on Peggy's door.

'You think what you like but you have no right to stop me. He is my father and you can't do anything. I will see him, whenever I wish. I will see him tomorrow and find somewhere else to stay and spend every day with him. I am his daughter and you . . .'

She turned away without finishing the sentence, not even knowing what she was going to say, and went to bed and slept at once.

She woke to the light being switched on. Peggy was standing in the doorway, grey-faced.

'We have to go to the hospital. Didn't you hear the phone?'

She had heard nothing. Peggy was incapable even of calling a taxi, she was shaking so much. It was almost three o'clock and Olive had to ring several numbers before she found one who would come, and that only as a favour because it was illness. They dressed and sat in their coats and waited and the buoys blinked on and off out at sea and they said no word to one another.

In the cold-smelling taxi they sat apart looking out on their respective sides, at the deserted streets. Only the lights of the hospital shone out from the top of the rise.

He had died ten minutes ago.

He looked utterly changed since she had seen him on the previous day – changed back. He was like himself again, the self of ten or more years before. His eyes were closed. There was no distressing, blank stare and his left side looked the same as his right, now, the arm straight and still. The blind was pulled down and there was a screen across the open doorway.

Olive took his hand and held it, kissed his cheek and then simply sat, resting with him. It was as if she had not rested or been still for years. He had always been able to soothe her, after some tormenting childhood nightmare or other fright, harsh words from her mother, and so he soothed her now. He had not known the truth about her, she had not been given the chance to tell him about Thea. Perhaps she would never have done so. Peggy was certain that he had been spared by death from knowledge of her shame. But in everyone else's eyes, having had an illegitimate child was shameful too. More so. Less?

She stroked his hand. Already the neatly cut fingernails were opaque, drained of blood and pale as bone.

'I don't know,' she said to him. 'I don't know anything, except what I feel, and how can anyone know more?'

She lifted his hand and kissed the back of it and felt the weight of tissue and flesh and bone, and in the weight there was only the total absence of all quickness, all life.

She expected Peggy to stay for some time, and so she wandered down the corridor and out of the quiet building. But Peggy joined her within a few minutes.

'I thought you'd left. I thought you couldn't face it.'

'He's my father. What could I not face? But you didn't have to leave so quickly. I can wait as long as you want.'

'He's gone. There's nothing to say, is there?'

She took a step or two away from Olive, fumbling in her bag for cigarettes.

Dear Miss Dauncey,

I am travelling back on Wednesday, after my father's funeral and will be in school the next day and for the rest of the term.

All good wishes.

Sincerely,

Olive Piper

28

Dear O,

Sorry for taking such an age to reply – we've been moving house and can you imagine what that's like with two children under five and both with chickenpox? We haven't gone far but we have to rent, and although we're not in such a nice area – or house – at least we're saving money. I wish I could see you. I miss our old chats.

As to your news, I don't know what to say really. It's something I've never understood at all and I suppose I believe nature meant us to be two halves, male/female. That's the way it seems to be, isn't it? I wonder if you're just having a bit of a crisis and that has confused you? I don't know. But I'm pretty sure it will pass, you'll meet someone and have a family and this will just all resolve itself.

Of course I'm not condemning or disapproving – you're not bad at all, but I think you probably need some guidance. Wish I were nearer and we could talk. You're welcome up here at any time though it's always chaos and there's only the old sofa but I'd love to see you. And good luck, O, I'll think of you and hope you get it all straight.

Love from your friend,

Margaret

Dear Olive,

Thank you for your note. It has been a difficult time for you and I hope you are up to coming in to school. I would like to see you first thing on Thursday morning, after assembly, if you are able to do that.

Sincerely,

Avril Dauncey

She had saved the envelope addressed in Thea's hand until last, when she had unpacked, made tea, savouring the moments of anticipation. She plumped up and rearranged the cushions on her armchair, took off her shoes. Poured out and drank. Then she slit open the envelope.

Olive, my dear,

I don't know when you are coming back but if it is before the end of term, and you go into school, be warned. AD will ask to see you. I have already been 'summoned', and as a result, I am not returning for the rest of this school year – officially, because I am 'ill'. You will be asked to do the same, but in your case, because you are only a probationer still, there may be more to it. I don't know. Nothing has been said. But be prepared.

In view of all this, we should not see one another but I will, of course, be in touch. I hope things have not been too hard and that you are well. I am so sorry for my part in all this – it is my fault, and all my responsibility, and I should have known better,

Affectionately,
Thea

She read the letter and read it again, and again, but however many times she did so she could not manage to extract from it a single word either of love or of comfort. Why had she written so coldly? And why on school-headed paper, other than to conceal her address? What did she mean about having to feign illness, and by telling her she had to be prepared?

She started a reply half a dozen times, and tore up each attempt. She did not want letters between them, she wanted to see Thea, to talk, to be close.

She was distraught, and hurt, and shocked, and she barely slept, and got up and left the flat far earlier than she needed to, so that there were no girls in yet. The cleaners were still mopping the corridors. As she went in, she saw Miss Dauncey ahead of her, brief-case in hand, pleated skirt swaying slightly as she walked, and seeing her purposeful back, Olive almost turned and fled. But it was the Head who turned. Stopped. Waited. Smiled. She looked perfectly welcoming.

'Good, we can talk now before anyone else button-holes me. Even my secretary won't be in for another half-hour. Do come in. I expect you might like some coffee? Making a pot for myself is the first thing I do. Do sit down, please.'

Normal. Pleasant. Friendly – as much as she ever was. But she was not the opposite either. You could tell nothing. She gave away nothing. Coffee. Hot. Strong. No biscuits.

'First of all, how are you? It is an awful shock, losing a parent. Very hard especially when it's so sudden.'

'Yes . . . it was quite bleak. And my stepmother is finding it very hard. But I am really all right, thank you.'

A look. Assessing her. Shrewd. She set down her cup.

'Olive, this has been your first year as a teacher. You are young but you have made an extremely good start. You're a natural teacher – you're enthusiastic and well organised, you cover the groundwork well but you also take your lessons in exciting directions – you engage the girls, you carry them with you. You open their eyes. I expect good exam results.'

She shifted in her chair. Glanced out of the window. Glanced at Olive but the glance did not linger.

'I must tell you that speaking entirely personally, your private life, shall we call it, does not concern me – and I mean in any sense. Of course I have known teachers who have had close friendships with others – of their own sex – even lived together. In my view that is their business. But it is always necessary, especially in our profession, to be discreet. A lot of people are intolerant. The majority probably do not share my view. And I am very sorry that you have not been entirely discreet – I have spoken about this to Thea and perhaps you know by now that she is off school until the end of the term. But she will of course return in September.'

She paused, looking directly at Olive.

'Have you spoken to her?'

'No. She wrote me a letter which I didn't fully understand. I still don't.'

'I see.'

'Miss Dauncey, what has happened?'

'I had a visit from a parent – the mother of a girl in the school – I am not prepared to give you any names. Her daughter had told her that she had, well, become aware of your close friendship with Thea – apparently she had seen you together. Once, coming out of your house very late at night – and don't worry, I did ask what the girl was doing out herself. I had a not altogether satisfactory answer but that is beside the point.'

'Am I not allowed to have visitors after nine o'clock? Rather as it was in college.'

'Please don't be sarcastic. I am trying to make this less difficult. Olive, there has been talk before now. A member of staff expressed concern.'

'A member . . . ?'

'As I said . . .'

'People spying and causing trouble but I am not allowed to know who?'

'No. You are not. And I have not simply been listening to staffroom gossip. I do have eyes and ears of my own.'

'But we . . .'

No. She could not say any more, partly because her throat seemed to have closed over and she was fighting back tears of anger, but mainly because she knew that there was no point in arguing or trying to defend herself. Them. It was all decided. All settled.

'What will happen now?'

'I'm afraid you will not be asked to return at the end of your probationary year. I simply do not feel it would be in anyone's best interests.'

'I see. I don't know what I shall do.'

'Move right away, to another part of the country entirely. Apply for jobs there. I will be happy to give you an excellent reference as far as your teaching abilities are concerned. You are good and you could go on to become exceptional. I simply will not mention anything else – besides, what is there to mention? If I were asked a direct question – but I doubt if I would be. You left because you wanted to move to – well, wherever it is you choose to go.'

The corridors outside had been coming alive with the sound of footsteps, with voices.

Miss Dauncey stood. 'I am very sorry about this.'

There was nothing that she could say in reply.

'Shall I stay until the end of term?'

'I think it best not. Leave now – use the side door. You can come in at the weekend to collect your things – there is always someone here on Saturday mornings who will be able to let you in.'

She held out her hand. Slim, cool hand. A slim, cool woman. The handshake was firm and swift.

'Why don't you just wait here and slip out when everyone has gone into assembly?'

She did not look back because she did not care, although she was both angry and humiliated. But it did not matter. The school. The pupils. Lessons. Staff. Parents. None of it mattered, only Thea. She must see Thea. Once she did, once they were together, everything would resolve itself, and be clear and very simple. Distance had blurred and confused everything. There was misunderstanding. None of it mattered. All of it would be seen for what it really was. Which was nothing.

She paused at a café which had just opened, realising that she was hungry. She ordered coffee and two eggs on toast, and sat, the only customer so far, at a window table overlooking the street and the ruined city wall, the side of the Abbey.

Thea would return to school as usual in the autumn, or so it was assumed. But there was no need. They could find somewhere, go a long way, and get jobs but in different schools, and live together distant from either. No one here would know. No one there would know. It was very straightforward.

29

S HE HAD her thick hair cut that afternoon, into a swinging bob. She also found a bottle of Tweed perfume, given to her by Peggy, and which Thea had said she liked. She felt calm. When she caught the bus to Thea's village she felt in control of herself and her emotions for the first time since seeing the Head.

It was quiet country they travelled through. The wayside grasses were bleached pale, the trees dusty-looking. There was nothing dramatic. It was ordinary rural England and she felt warmly towards it and realised how little of it she had seen since first coming here, how unaware of it all. She had turned to John Donne the night before, looking for her feelings.

> *Only our love hath no decay;*
> *This no tomorrow hath, nor yesterday,*

Running it never runs from us away,
But truly keeps his first, last, everlasting day.

The words, and others, danced in her head, and stencilled themselves on the window between her eyes and the view, so that she was never afterwards able to look at meadows and hedgerows and gentle hills without seeing the impress of the words upon them.

She got off outside the village post office. It was empty. She bought a packet of mints and a bar of Fry's chocolate cream, Thea's weakness, and always safe, as she said, if she left one around, because Olive disliked it. They had never given one another anything other than small presents like this. Later, Thea had said. One day. Lifetime presents.

'Are there ever any houses to let in the village?'

The woman behind the counter gave her a questioning look. How she assessed Olive, it seemed, might influence her reply.

'There are. Sometimes.'

'Now?'

'I know 2 The Green is waiting for a tenant. And Oddstock Cottage, but that one's still in a terrible mess after Mr Parsons died. He hadn't left home for over twenty years and it shows. There was talk of Wren House coming vacant. Very nice, but large of course, if it was for yourself. 2 The Green would suit.'

'Thank you. That's very helpful. Now, I've got to call on a friend – Miss Pengelly?'

'At number 3 The Green, which you would expect to be next door but is actually the far end and don't ask me for an explanation of that.'

She walked slowly down the short main street, lined with terraced cottages on either side. The road curved and there was the green. Iron swings. A slide. The cottages were along the north side, stone-built, fenced, with long, profusely flowering front gardens. Bean wigwams. Sweet peas clambering. Last roses.

Number 2. Why had Thea not mentioned it? Perhaps she didn't know.

She could live there. She looked over the gate. Neglected front garden. A side path to a gate in an arch. No one about. She wanted to live there, now, today.

A woman passed on a bicycle. Glanced. Good morning. Lovely morning. A cat sat in the sunlight on the path in front of her. Crown imperials, like the garden in *Alice in Wonderland*. She longed to go in. Walked on.

She reached the end of the row and saw Thea's car. Stopped, her heart thumping, then scurrying. Thea. She put her hand in her pocket and touched the bar of chocolate cream. It was a larger cottage, because it was at the end. A row of pea sticks. More sweet peas in abundant flower. A row of sunflowers against the fence. Hollyhocks. Thea.

She took a breath and walked up the path. She dared not look in the windows.

No one came to her knock. She waited. Perhaps they were at the back, in the garden there. She knocked again.

The door was opened almost at once, startling her. Opened by Sylvia Neale. Olive took a step back.

The smile was an odd one, not welcoming, nor friendly, but small and knowing. She held the door and called over her shoulder.

'Thea? Darling – your girl is here to see you.'

30

I<small>T WAS</small> a small grey stone building, like so many of its kind, with an asphalt playground, tall windows, and three steps up to the main door.

But not so many of the others had such a view. It stretched gently away from the top of the slope on which the school stood, an open plain of meadows and lanes, with low hills rising to higher hills and, beyond them, a distant Cumbrian mountain, and in some weathers, some lights, the mountain became violet, and seemed nearer. You could stretch out your hand and touch it.

Across the green plain ran the river, broad and curving like a snake as it went, sometimes sparkling silver, more often grey.

The view had taken her breath away the first time she had seen it and it did so still. She had been here almost a year. Easegarth St Aidan's Church of England Primary School.

It was spring. It was May. But although the sun shone, it was chased across the landscape by the breeze that always blew here, running ahead of the shadows, which caught it and hid it and sped on.

She stood now, beside the iron handrail leading to the front door. All around her, small colourful figures, like children in a Flemish painting, played, ran about, skipped, jump-roped, or squatted in huddles of three or four, around a set of jack stones thrown onto the ground.

She had done as she had been advised. She had come as far away from the old place, the old school, as she could, in reply to an advertisement. But not one for a teacher. She had recoiled from the idea of teaching, though perhaps, in ten or twenty years, it might draw her back.

Classroom Assistant and School Helper for Mixed Infant C of E school. Experience useful but not essential. Must love young children and rural life in this remote farming community in the north of England.

She had seen the notice, and ignored it, seen it again the following week, and the one after that, and so on for almost two months. So they had found no one, then, or no one suitable.

And then she realised that she was the one and she must apply. She was the one who would be suitable.

It seemed so. She had loved the place, the people, the children, the building, the job, from the moment she had arrived, and been happy at once, as she had never believed she could ever possibly be happy again.

The rest of her life, the distant and the near past, were so far away they might never have been, though she dreamed of them sometimes. Dreamed of poems taught, and recited them in her sleep. Donne. Herbert. Chaucer. John Skelton. John Clare.

Dreamed of the narrow lane leading to her flat and of the long cool corridor in the school.

Dreamed of the bright apartment. Dreamed of her father. Dreamed of the sea.

But although she thought of her a great deal, she never dreamed of Thea.

Her thoughts skidded away. What she had been. What had happened. What she had done.

Love.

Shock.

Betrayal.

The need to unpick everything she had believed and trusted in.

She was renting a farm cottage two miles from the school, and cycled to it most days in fair weather. The winter had been harsh so she had walked, but some days could not even do that, and had been forced to stay at home, like everyone else. In the worst of late January, the school had closed for two weeks, the snow had been so deep, the cold so intense, the gales so violent.

What was the sound she was listening to and which had become so familiar that, like the birdsong or the keening of the wind, she scarcely noticed?

Shouts. Shrieks. Cries. Calls. Laughter. Singing. Chanting. More shouts, blown away on the wind and returned again by the hills.

Playground noise, she thought, was the same here today as it had been two or three hundred years ago, the same across the world.

Two small girls wandered by, arms round one another, whispering.

Two small boys raced past, flailing their arms, making whirring sounds.

And then a different cry, louder and more urgent.

A small group had gathered round the one who had tumbled, running too fast and skidding.

He lay on the ground, surrounded by others, bending over him, anxious, interested.

She went quickly.

'William Dove, Miss Piper, he's got blood and everything.'

William Dove, stocky, compact, dark-haired, not yet six years old, lay crying, his nose running, his knee scraped, gravel and blood mingling.

Olive knelt down and took his hand. 'All right, William, it's going to be fine. I know, it's horrid to come crashing down like that, it gives you an awful shock, as well as hurting. Let me have a look and then we'll get you up and inside. Melanie, will you please go and ask Mrs Runton to come here?'

His small face was white, and scoured with tears.

And suddenly, he was James. He was James grown older, and injured and needing her, and this time, she was here, beside him, tending him, not in some other place, where he could not reach her, where strangers had him, where everything sounded and smelled and felt different.

She stroked William Dove's hand and he gripped hers and snuffled back the next stream of tears.

'There . . . good boy. We'll soon make you feel better. Poor you.'

Poor James.

She shook herself. Not James.

And everything else was remote and distant and did not matter. Did not matter at all.

'Hello . . . what's happened?'

Mrs Runton. Jenny. Infant teacher. Loving. Loyal. Devoted to every child and all the children.

Together, they helped him up and he leaned on Olive and went hopping beside her into the school, and the playground noise rose again, and boys wheeled and spun round and girls shrieked and giggled and the sun shone and small clouds raced like hares across the fields below, and everyday life went on.